THE CHRONICLES OF THE VIRAGO

THE NOVUS: BOOK 1

MICHAEL BIALYS

To Misty
My wife, my love and my muse, if not for her there would be no Makenna,
Emilyne or Noah.
She is my Virago.

.

vi·ra·go (və-rä′gō, -rä′-, vîr′ə-gō)
[Latin *virāgō*, from *vir*, man.] A large, strong, courageous woman.

A virago is a woman who demonstrates exemplary and heroic qualities.

PROLOGUE

The worst thing that Good could do to Evil was ignore it.
The Dark One could not stand being ignored. The Evil One
had tried to get his attention, goad him into battle,
Fight him as he had done since the beginning of time. The
Light would not engage The Dark:
This only served to frustrate the Dark One, infuriate him.
In fact, Evil took his revenge upon the earth
and still Good let Evil run rampant
for many millennia.
The Light would not confront The Dark.
Not until it was time…

1

THE GIFT

He sat in his London penthouse office, Number 66, 6th Street. This was the corporate headquarters of the multinational Natasi Industries. Sensing the arrival of the Gift, he smiled. Somehow atmospheric conditions seemed lighter that day, indicating the Gift's impending arrival. Though the saccharine air made him physically nauseous, he was nonetheless in a good mood. The war had finally begun.

In his right hand he played with a metal pawn he had plucked from the chessboard on the marble credenza. He rolled the piece in his hand, contemplating his next move. He enjoyed the sensation of the cold metal running through his fingers. The pawn was crafted from pure platinum at a cost of £100,000.00. Sir Seaton came from old money... *very* old money. He was one of the richest men in the world, and he had no problem enjoying his wealth or displaying it. After all, money *was* the root of all evil.

As he considered his next move, the office intercom chimed.

"Sir?" a voice asked. "The Prime Minister is on the line. He'd like to know if you are still available for high tea today at the House of Lords."

"Yes Ms. Creante, confirm that appointment," answered Seaton, "and summon Ms. Chevious. I want to see both of you in my office immediately."

Moments later, the door opened and two women entered Sir Seaton's office, which consisted of twelve-foot-high vaulted ceilings festooned with walls of handsome dark cherry wood. Behind him stood a wall of glass, overlooking the Thames and providing a sweeping view of the London Skyline. The remaining walls were lined with bookshelves upon which sat books, magazines, periodicals, and newspapers, all impeccably ordered and catalogued. Sir Seaton loved to read, most especially about himself. He sat behind his black granite-topped desk, enjoying the undertones of *Faust*, playing at a low ambient volume in the background.

Seaton watched dispassionately as Ms. Creante and Ms. Chevious made their way toward his massive desk. They walked in silence, their high heels muted by the blood-red Berber carpet.

"Good morning, ladies," Seaton said, surreptitiously marveling at their beauty. Both women were stunning, but quite opposite in their appearance. Ms. Creante stood at a willowy six feet tall, with waist-length blonde hair. Her ice-blue eyes and high cheekbones gave her a classically Nordic appearance.

Ms. Chevious, by comparison, was equally tall, but her features were softer and more rounded. Her perfectly straight black hair hung like a curtain around her face, the ends just touching her shoulders. Her eyes were a deep green fringed with strikingly long lashes, and her full, bee-stung lips were pursed slightly in a pout. The women stood shoulder to shoulder, each wearing perfectly tailored Chanel business suits.

Sir Seaton did not stand but leaned forward in his chair.

"Ladies, I have felt its presence," he said. "It has begun. There is no time to spare. I must find the Gift. Do you understand what I am asking?"

The women stared at him stoically. Seaton sized them both up for a moment, then gave an almost nigh imperceptible nod.

"It is time. Release the Hounds."

2

THE INITIATION

Makenna gulped down her third glass of water, then climbed back into bed. She pulled her blankets up to her chin, promptly kicked them off again, and sat up. Her mother suddenly appeared in the doorway.

"Makenna Grace Gold!" her mother exclaimed. "Why are you still awake? It's almost 10:30, and you know it's a school night."

"I know," Makenna said apologetically. "I'm sorry, Mom. I'm just so excited about the Science Fair tomorrow!"

The expression on her mother's face softened. "I know you are, sweetie. But remember, you won't be at your best if you're exhausted. Now get some sleep. I love you, baby."

"Love you too, Mom," Makenna said, smiling at her mother. "Goodnight. And tell Dad I love him too!"

Makenna's mother quietly closed the door, leaving the room pitch black. Makenna lay back and snuggled under the covers, trying to make herself sleepy, but she couldn't stop thoughts of her Science Fair project from running through her mind. She had worked so hard on it, and her Dad had helped her. Makenna was certain her presentation would be amazing. No one had ever done anything like a crystallization project before.

Makenna had been growing her own homemade sugar crystals for over two weeks. As a surprise, she was going to hand out her homemade samples to her classmates and teachers. She couldn't wait to see how they reacted. Candy as science! Makena just knew Heather Stern, allegedly the smartest girl in the class and Makenna's personal nemesis, would be wildly jealous.

As that happy thought crossed her mind, Makenna finally gave in to the drowsiness that crept up on her. As she finally closed her eyes and fell asleep, Makenna Grace Gold had no reason to suspect that this night would be the most unexpected and remarkable night she had ever known.

BREE DELPHINE GIGGLED MISCHIEVOUSLY as she flew figure-eights in front of the bedroom mirror. She never tired of watching the trail of gold fairy dust form luminescent shapes in the dark.

Dee Delphine, Fairy First Class, watched her cousin scornfully, then decided to put a quick end to Bree's antics. Dee launched herself directly into Bree's path, flying straight at her as if to force a mid-air collision, then breaking off at the last moment.

"Breeana Delphine!" Dee Delphine whispered, her wings beating silently as she hovered in front of her cousin, "We are not here to marvel at your ridiculous Fairobatics. We are here to initiate the Protector."

Bree opened her mouth to issue a retort, but before she could speak the human girl in the bed below them began to stir.

"Quiet, both of you!" exclaimed Marigold, hovering silently over the foot of the bed. "The girl must not wake before we begin. And I'm certain you-know-who is watching," she added. "If you two don't stop these fooleries, you'll both earn yourselves a wing downgrade!"

"Sorry," the fairy cousins said in unison, their voices earnestly repentant.

Marigold Frith, Fairy Prelate, smiled, pleased that her scolding had achieved its desired end.

It was time. Makenna had to be told. She was The Protector, she whom history would remember as The Virago, Warrior of Warriors.

"Ladies, join me please." Marigold nodded to her companions. Bree and Dee obediently flew to Marigold and hovered beside the Fairy Prelate over the foot of Makenna's bed.

The trio of fairies took a moment to examine Makenna's bedroom before beginning their appointed task. The fairies had to make sure that no one would witness what they were about to do.

Satisfied the room was secure, Marigold took a final moment to marvel at Makenna's innocence and beauty, knowing that from this moment forward, she would be innocent no more.

It was a great honor to be here with the Virago, but Marigold couldn't help feeling a sense of sadness. The human girl, just twelve Earth years in age, was beguilingly beautiful. Her long chestnut hair lay in soft tendrils across the pillow as she slept. Her face was that of an angel, serene and dignified, with a little dimple in her chin. Marigold Frith, Fairy Prelate, allowed a tiny dutiful sigh to escape her lips before saying, "Ladies, it is time. Let us begin."

The three fairies began their elemental dance, one that had rarely been done since the very creation of time. It had been centuries since any fairy had danced these steps of the elements. Now, on this night, it was time.

Each fairy flew in silent synchronicity, trailed by a stream of light, weaving around one another in an elaborate crisscross pattern. The three interwoven light trails glowed in the dark like a radiant braided blade, slicing through the black. It was no mere trick of the eye; the braided strands of light began to fuse together in the air. The incandescent pattern was transmuting, not simply taking the shape of a sword but becoming one. This was the Ancient Weapon. A sword of unspeakable power, forged not from steel, but comprised entirely of light and hope, and the dreams of all who lived. The Ancient Weapon had but one purpose – to defend and represent all that was good in the universe.

Over the millennia, anyone honored enough to wield the weapon was also privileged to choose its earthly form and to name it. In one of its more famous incarnations, it was known as Excalibur. David, King of the

Hebrews and one of the first warriors, chose to wield the weapon as a sling. Makenna would have to find a form and a name for the weapon that best suited her. The weapon was bonded to its owner.

Marigold took in the sight of the shimmering sword, wondering how this young human would learn to wield it in the way of a warrior.

The blade of light glowed brighter and brighter, until Makenna's entire room was illuminated, bathed in the light of hope. Makenna shifted beneath the blanket, then her eyes blinked open. She squinted and put her hands up to shield her eyes from the brilliance of the lighted sword.

Am I dreaming? she thought.

Surely she had to be, but it was unlike any dream Makenna had ever had. What did it mean? What was this gleaming sword that seemed to be made from the rays of light that shone through it?

Like a crystal, Makenna thought. *That's it! I'm dreaming about my Science Fair project!*

Makenna opened her eyes wider, no longer finding the light so painful. As her eyes adjusted, she heard a little buzzing sound, as if a fly or a bee had flown by her ear.

"Wake up! Wake up, young Protector," Makenna heard, just as she caught sight of a faint trail of light shooting past her like a tiny comet.

"Protector, you must wake up!" the voice repeated, gentle and urgent at the same time.

Makenna resisted. It took her long enough to fall asleep, by this point she just didn't want to wake up. She needed her sleep so she would be ready for the Science Fair. Makenna lay back on her pillow, pulling her comforter over her head.

Using a strength that belied her tiny size, Marigold pulled the comforter off Makenna's head.

"No, youngling. This is no time for sleep. The twins are almost here," Marigold urged in her little fairy voice.

Makenna relented. She sat up in bed, surrendering to this bizarre dream with its talking insects and swords of light. It's not as if she could ignore them.

Marigold flew to Makenna, hovering just a few inches from the girl's face. As Bree and Dee continued to make their crisscross orbits around the golden blade, Marigold began to speak. Still only half-awake, Makenna could not fail to realize that the voice addressing her was coming from this fairy, no bigger than a butterfly.

"I am Marigold Frith, Fairy Prelate," the fairy said, "and you, young one, are The Protector, she who will be remembered as the Virago: Warrior of Warriors."

Makenna stared at the fairy hovering in front of her, stunned and confused by what she was seeing and hearing.

"Tomorrow they will come, the twins, your brother and sister, a great Gift that will lead your world into its next age," the fairy continued. "They will lead this world out of despair and into a new age of hope and enlightenment. But the Evil One knows of their arrival, he has been anticipating it. The Dark One wants the twins destroyed, thereby putting an end to a new age, the next stage in your world's evolution. By destroying the twins, your world will be plummeted into a state of ultimate despair and destruction. The twin children are a Gift the likes of which have not been seen for many millennia. They are your future and they must be protected!"

Makenna felt herself drifting off again.

This dream is exhausting.

Marigold, sensing she was losing Makenna to fatigue, raised her voice to keep the youngster awake. She nodded and winked to Bree and Dee. In response, the two fairies began to fly faster, creating an irritating high-pitched whistle, guaranteed to annoy and awaken even the weariest of customers.

Makenna immediately opened her eyes and sat up in bed somewhat more attentively. She tried to say something, to ask one of the multitude of questions running through her mind. She moved her lips, but nothing came out.

Marigold continued, "Hush, now. There is only one answer to your questions. History has already written your destiny. For now, you only need know that you have been charged with the protection of the babies, your brother and sister, Hope Incarnate. Mind them well, Virago."

With that, Bree, Dee and Marigold motioned their arms toward Makenna in unison, sending the golden hovering blade flying towards her. The sword flew toward its new master, passing directly into her body, essentially bonding with her so that they would become one.

Makenna jumped, startled by the sight of the blade rushing toward her. She felt a sudden, incredible burst of energy as the blade fused with her. It was like nothing she had ever felt before. She felt alive with strength. In that moment, she felt as if she could answer every question her teacher had ever posed, while simultaneously beating all the boys in basketball. It was an indescribable, exhilarating feeling.

Just as quickly, the incredible surge of energy was gone, leaving her slumped in utter exhaustion. Makenna felt drained and nauseated, like she'd just run a 100-yard dash at top speed. Makenna lay back on her pillow, closed her eyes, and instantly fell into a deep sleep.

Marigold flew over the sleeping child's head, scattering fairy dust over the girl to ensure good dreams.

"Rest well, young Virago Warrior, for tomorrow the war begins." With that, the fairies disappeared, and the room went black. As if they had never been there.

3

THE BIRTH

At 6:30 a.m., Makenna's alarm sounded. She woke up feeling as if she hadn't slept at all.

She remembered her bizarre dream from the night earlier. *That dream must have tired me out. Glowing swords, talking fairies, that was one crazy dream. Yet it had felt so real.* Makenna could still remember almost every detail.

The door burst open. Makenna's father stood in the doorway, already fully dressed. He looked uncharacteristically panicked.

"Great! You're up!" He stumbled over the jamb of her bedroom door as he entered the room. "Get dressed, quickly ... oh, by the way, good morning, baby."

"Dad, what's the rush?" Makenna asked. "I don't have to be at school till 8:00."

"We're not going to school, sweetie," he answered. "It's time! Mom's ready to have the babies! We're going to the hospital, but it's too early to drop you off at school, so you're coming with. We're leaving in five minutes, so let's hit it."

Before Makenna had time to respond, her father had rushed from the room.

This is all so strange, Makenna thought. Marigold, the fairy from her dream had said the twins would be coming today. What was even stranger was the fact that Makenna remembered the name of the fairy in her dream.

"Could it have been real?" she asked herself. "The Protector, Virago, good vs. evil, fairies, and floating swords? No. It had to have been a dream".

Then something came to her. Marigold had said that the twins would be a boy and a girl. But Makenna's mother had known for months that her twins were both girls. That was enough for Makenna to convince herself that what she had experienced the night before was only a crazy, albeit very vivid dream. Relieved, she began to get dressed. In mere minutes, Makenna and her Mom and Dad were in the car on the way to the Hospital. Today it would be official: Makenna was going to be a big sister!

MAKENNA SAT PATIENTLY in the Huntington Memorial Hospital waiting area. It was a small room with two hard couches, several small wooden tables strewn with dozens of magazines, and a television hooked up to the ceiling in the corner. Makenna figured she might be there for quite a while, so she was glad she had brought books to read. She looked at the clock. She had only been in there for twenty minutes.

A nurse poked her head into the room. "You ok, sweetie? Your Dad asked me to check on you."

"Yes, I'm fine, thanks," Makenna answered, a little sheepishly.

The nurse seemed nice enough. She was pretty and fresh-faced. She reminded Makenna of her old friend Rachel, who had just moved away.

"You must be excited," the nurse said. "I hear your Mom's having twins. You're gonna be a big sister times two!"

Makenna's father ran into the waiting room, bounding past the young nurse to where Makenna was sitting. "Congratulations, big sister!"

He bent down to give Makenna a hug. "Already?" Makenna said.

"It was incredible," he answered. "We checked Mom in, got settled in her room, and before I knew what was happening the babies came! No waiting, no anesthetic and, according to your Mom, no pain at all! Not a thing went wrong, unless you count the fact it's not two girls, like the doctor thought. Congratulations! We have a boy and a girl!"

Makenna felt her stomach drop in disbelief.

The fairy was right. So, it wasn't a dream after all! she thought. "What's wrong, baby?" her father asked. "You look like you've just

seen a ghost."

"Nothing, Dad. I'm just... excited."

"Well good, grab all your stuff and come with me. Let's go visit your new brother and sister," he said, helping Makenna pack up her book bag.

"What are their names, Dad?" It was all happening so suddenly. "Mom and I were thinking Noah for the boy, and Emilyne for the girl.

Wait until you see them. They're beautiful." He beamed with pride.

Makenna followed her father down the hallway, past a nurse's desk and to a doorway already festooned with pink and blue balloons.

"This is her room," he said. Makenna lingered in the doorway, hesitantly.

"Is that you, baby?" Makenna heard her mother call. "Come on in and meet your new brother and sister!"

"Hi Mom. How are you feeling?" Makenna asked.

It was strange to see her mother in a hospital bed. Makenna was relieved to see her mother was all smiles. She was a beautiful woman, with her wavy ash blonde hair and sky-blue eyes, and when she smiled she became even lovelier. No one could witness the trademark Misty Gold smile and not smile in return. Makenna was thrilled to see her mother looking so happy. Her cheeks were flushed and rosy, she practically glowed.

From the time she was baby, Makenna could remember hearing people saying how pretty her mother was. Makenna always took that as a huge compliment, considering everybody also told her that she looked exactly like her Mom.

"I feel great, I didn't have any pain or anything," her mother said. "I hardly knew I was having the babies. I almost feel invigorated. The most difficult baby to manage was your Dad over there. He was a nervous wreck."

Makenna laughed.

"Now come here young lady, give me a kiss and say hello to your new brother and sister," her Mom said, pretending to be making an actual demand.

Makenna leaned over the hospital bed, kissed her mother on the cheek and peered down at the two babies sleeping peacefully on either side of her Mom's chest. They were perfect tiny little angels. They each had thin manes of blondish brown hair crowning their heads. They had the smallest little noses and rosebud lips. The only way Makenna could tell that one was a girl and the other a boy was because one was wrapped in blue and the other was wrapped in pink.

The baby boy was lying on her mother's left side and the girl on the right side. Makenna carefully studied her new siblings. They were so small, and they looked so peaceful as they slept. The baby boy stirred and opened his eyes briefly, looking up at his big sister. Makenna could have sworn that he smiled at her. He closed his eyes and went back to sleep.

She was hooked. She didn't even understand it, but she instantly loved those babies. To Makenna they were the most beautiful things she'd ever seen, and she was so proud to be their big sister. She still wasn't quite sure what had happened to her the night before, but dream or no dream, Makenna knew she would never let anyone hurt these babies. Never.

"I love them, Mom. I already love them," Makenna said.

"I know, sweetie, that's just how it is," her mother replied. "It's nature. I love them, just like from the first moment I set eyes on you, I loved you too."

Something in her mother's voice made Makenna look up. "What's wrong Mom? Why are you crying?"

"Happy tears, Makenna. Happy tears."

4

THE INITIATE

Makenna sat in her Dad's car, thinking about her new brother and sister. She couldn't stop thinking about how cute they were. She kept playing with their names in her head, Noah and Emilyne, Emilyne and Noah, Noah and Emi, Emi and Noah. She didn't want to leave the hospital, but her Dad said it would be best for her to go to school. Her mother promised Makenna that she could come back that night and hold the babies again. At this point, she didn't care about the Science Fair; all she could think about was those babies.

"We're here," announced her Dad as he pulled his car into the school parking lot. "Now, do you have all your stuff for the Science Fair?"

"Yes, Dad."

"Got your crystal candies to hand out?"

"Yes, Dad," she answered, sounding very much in control of her situation.

"Okay, okay. I'll pick you up at 3:30 and we'll head back to the hospital. Give me a kiss."

She kissed her father on the cheek, then gathered her book bag and opened the car door. "Love you, Dad."

"Love you too. Have a great day... big sister." He beamed with pride.

Makenna smiled as she closed the car door. She was a big sister now, and she loved the sound of it.

She had missed the first few periods of school, and her classmates were out on the playground for morning recess. As she headed for the office to sign in, she heard it. That voice, the one that could make you wish you could crawl into a hole.

"Well look who decided to show up," sneered Heather Stern. "We thought for sure you were gonna chicken out of the Science Fair."

There she was, perfect little Heather Stern. Blonde, blue-eyed, flawless Heather Stern. Heather was regarded as both the smartest and the most stuck-up girl in the class. Heather's father was some super-important executive at a film studio. She had been in a bunch of commercials and had even done some small TV roles, and gloated about it constantly. She always wore the best clothes and let everybody know much money her family had.

She was flanked on either side by her tagalongs, Michelle Bishel and Elise Green. Heather stepped in front of Makenna, blocking her path to the office.

"Sorry Heather, but I'm here, and I'm gonna win this Science Fair," answered Makenna, meeting Heather's challenging gaze with her own.

"I've already heard about your little crystal candies, Makenna, and I sure hope it beats out my homemade ice cream maker, and my report on the history of ice cream," declared Heather loudly.

The Tagalongs punctuated Heather's statement with giggles.

Makenna flushed with embarrassment, which quickly turned to anger. *Patience, Makenna. Don't let them see that they are getting to you.* "You know, Heather, I had a feeling you were doing a food project,"

Makenna said calmly.

"Really, and how's that?" asked Michelle in her most sarcastic tone. "Let's just say that she must have been testing a lot of her product

over the last few weeks, and it really, really shows," Makenna retorted, bulging out her cheeks as she answered.

All three girls stood there dumbfounded, mouths agape. Makenna stepped around the girls and continued along to the office. As she walked away, she decided to add one last retort. "Close your mouths, girls. Heather's likely to shove some of her ice cream into it, and then you'll start looking like her."

All three girls let out a shocked gasp. "Not nice, Protector," a voice said.

What was that? Makenna wondered, looking around. She didn't see anyone.

"You're going to have to learn to be a bit more charitable in the future, Virago," the mysterious voice said. "Now meet us behind the school, at the utility doors."

It was as if someone was whispering in her head. It was eerie and annoying at the same time.

"Now, Virago! You must come now!" the voice demanded.

Curious, Makenna instinctively obeyed. Rather than continue to the office to sign in, she proceeded to the utility door.

The utility room was where the school caretaker stored all his equipment and cleansers. It was in an isolated part of the building where students and faculty didn't often go. Makenna stood in front of the utility door as she had been called on to do. She shivered, unsure if she was frightened or just cold. After a minute or two, she began to feel foolish, wondering why she was standing there.

There's no voice now. Maybe it was just my imagination.

She was very tired, after all. It had been quite an exciting but exhausting morning with the new babies.

As she was about to give up and go to the office, she was stopped in her tracks. Not three inches from her face hovered what can only be described as a full on, bona fide, authentic, Tinkerbell-style fairy!

"Hold, Warrior!" the fairy demanded. "We must speak, and this time you will not have the guise of sleep to distract you."

Makenna's knees went weak, her stomach felt queasy, and her legs gave out from under her. Before she could fall, something caught her arms and pulled her up. On each side of her were two more fairies, supporting her elbows. Makenna looked in disbelief to her left and right as both Bree and Dee Delphine smiled at her, slightly bowing their heads.

"Ma'am," they said in unison.

Makenna was speechless, her mouth hanging open as she stared back and forth at the fairies.

"Get hold of yourself, Warrior of Warriors. You will have far worse challenges than this to overcome," declared the third fairy, floating at Makenna's eye level. "I am Marigold Frith, Fairy Prelate, and I have been charged with your mentoring and training, Virago. The fairy on your left is Dee Delphine, and the one on your right is Bree Delphine, cousins and Fairies First Class. They will be assisting me with your training, as I can see I will need all the help I can get."

Both Bree and Dee again responded by bowing their heads at Makenna in a slight curtsy motion.

"Ma'am?" asked Bree from Makenna's right. "Do you feel you can stand on your own quite yet? You are getting a bit heavy."

"Breeana Delphine! She's the Virago, you should be honored to hold her up!" hissed Dee.

Marigold interrupted, "Ladies, please!"

"I can stand on my own now, thank you." Makenna composed herself, focusing her attention on the Fairy Prelate hovering in front of her.

Makenna couldn't help staring at Marigold. It was hard to make out her exact features because of the glow shimmering around her tiny body. She was about three inches tall, with long flaxen hair that framed her pixie face in wisps. Her fine features were complemented by a small upturned nose and a tulip-shaped mouth. Her ears tapered to delicate points. Her butterfly wings looked translucent and beat rapidly like those of a hummingbird.

Makenna was struck with how closely Marigold resembled the story-book fairies that she had grown up reading about. She admired Marigold's beautiful glowing wings, which seemed to be three times the size of her body. As quickly as they flapped to hold up the little fairy, they were nonetheless perfectly graceful. Dust flew from the wings as they beat, leaving a slight iridescent gleam in the air.

Fairy dust! Makenna thought.

Bree and Dee were not so different in form, but Dee had a reddish shade to her hair, which fell just above her dainty shoulders, and Bree had chestnut brown hair cut slightly shorter than Dee's. All of them had large light eyes, and a blue-greenish glow that emanated from their irises. All three fairies were dressed in what appeared to be flowing, silken dresses.

As difficult as it was to believe, Makenna knew that this was no dream, and she was surrounded by three beautiful and very persistent fairies.

Marigold spoke. "The twins have arrived, just as I told you. You, young Warrior, are charged with their protection. The Dark One will eventually learn where they are, and when he does, he will come after them. The twins must be protected at all costs."

"The Dark One?" asked Makenna, hoping she didn't sound as nervous as she felt.

"Yes," Marigold replied. "The Dark One is the embodiment of evil. He desires nothing more than to see this world forever plunged into darkness and despair."

Oh, is that all I have to do? Makenna thought sarcastically. *Just stop some evil guy who is planning to end the world?* "I'm only twelve years old! How exactly am I supposed to stop him?"

"Do not worry, child," Marigold answered, kindness in her eyes. "Your predecessors were also very young when they were chosen. David was a mere child when he slew Goliath and became King of the Israelites. Arthur wasn't much older when he pulled the Sword from the Stone and formed his famous Knights of the round table. They were chosen just as you were, to protect and ensure hope and enlightenment. To do this, Makenna, you must defend your brother and sister against the evil that seeks to harm them."

"Battle evil?" Makenna exclaimed in disbelief. "I'm not even that good in gym!"

"Please, child, listen well," Marigold said. "You have been chosen. It is done. Do not question it. "Though it may not seem so to you now, it is a great honor. Few in the history of creation have ever had such trust bestowed upon them."

"But...I mean, shouldn't my Mom and Dad be the ones to do this? That's what parents do, right? Protect their children?"

"Your parents have been charged with other duties. They will teach the children love and compassion. They will equip them naturally with the tools that they need to carry this world into the next age. Because of their crucial role, they, too, will be in danger, and you must safeguard them as well."

Makenna's knees went wobbly again. Bree and Dee quickly flew in again to steady her.

"But ... I..." Makenna began, stumbling over her own words. "Me, a twelve-year old girl, must protect my new brother and sister, my own parents, and the future of the world? I didn't ask for this. I don't want this. I don't know the first thing about being a... what did you call it? Virogah?"

"Oh, she's a quick one," said Dee.

"It's no wonder he picked her, she's quite clever," agreed Bree.

"But that's just it," Makenna said, fighting the urge to burst into tears. "I think there's been a mistake. I don't want this. I don't know what to do, I'm not supposed to be your... Virago!" She said the word correctly that time, but the word stuck in her throat as she said it.

"Tell that to your new siblings, child," Bree suggested.

"Whether you like it or not Makenna, there is no mistake," Marigold said. "You *are* the Virago. You were carefully chosen for a very good reason. You must tell no one of this. Be careful who you trust. The Evil One is the Lord of Lies and Deceit. He may use others to try and trick you. He will stop at nothing to destroy the twins. Not even your parents can know. They must appear as normal loving parents to provide the proper nurturing environment in which the babies can thrive. Do you understand everything I've said, Makenna?" She hovered in the air, awaiting a response.

Makenna just stood, staring, speechless.

5

THE HOUNDS RELEASED

Sir Seaton sat across from his minions and calmly directed them to the private elevator in his office.

"You'll need to use my private lift. You're going to the sub-basement." A nefarious glint flashed across his eyes as he said it.

"Yes, Sir Seaton," answered Ms. Creante.

Ms. Chevious simply smiled impishly and nodded at her boss.

Sir Seaton watched the women step into the elevator. Seaton smiled as the doors closed behind them. He looked down at the pawn that he had been rolling between his fingers. The platinum chess piece had melted into a shapeless lump of molten slag. It seemed his excitement and anticipation had gotten the better of him. Realizing what he had done, he chuckled.

In the elevator, Ms. Creante and Ms. Chevious were having a polite exchange with the elevator operator.

"Good morning, Roger," Ms. Creante said.

"Morning, ma'am, how's it with you ladies this fine morning?" answered the operator in a strong Cockney accent.

"Just fine, Roger. You're looking well," answered Ms. Creante.

"Well, thank you, ma'am. Things have been a little bit up an' down lately, but I've no complaints, ma'am."

Roger was Sir Seaton's private lift operator. He was doing quite well for a man who had been dead for over 600 years. Roger was a mere skeleton, clad in traditional elevator operator's uniform. The uniform was obviously a little loose fitting on him, given the fact that he lacked muscle tissue, organs and skin.

"Floor please, ma'am?" asked Roger.

"Oh, my apologies, Roger. Sub-basement please," answered Ms. Creante.

"Not a problem, ma'am. Special trip today, eh ladies?"

"Quite special, Roger," answered a very pleased Ms. Chevious.

Roger pressed a red button on the elevator panel. The elevator jolted as it accelerated downwards at an unfathomable speed. The speed was necessary, considering the sub-basement was about 3,000 miles below the Earth's surface.

The ladies smiled at each other in anticipation of what was to come. The elevator trip would take some time, but it was worth it. The ladies sat down on two leather recliners provided for passengers taking long trips.

Not one word was spoken for the rest of the thirty-minute journey down into the sub-basement. Eventually, the elevator jolted again as it decelerated to a stop.

"Sub-basement, ladies. Enjoy your trip," Roger announced.

The elevator doors now glowed a deep red color, and when they opened, the elevator filled with steam, heat and the sound of bubbling lava.

"Thank you, Roger," answered Ms. Creante.

Ms. Chevious smiled and winked at Roger. Both ladies then disembarked the elevator, unaffected by the 2000-degree temperatures that engulfed them.

The ladies walked forward along a pathway made of glowing molten rock, seemingly impervious to the flowing lava and flames all around them. They did not stop until they reached a mammoth set of metal doors, five stories high and almost as wide. The massive iron doors were designed to swing only one way. They let people in, but didn't let them out.

To make certain no one got past the doorway from the inside, the fabled three-headed dog, Cerberus, stood guard.

Although Cerberus looked small next to the towering door he guarded, the three-headed dog himself stood at twenty feet high. The creature had the ferocious features of an aberrant pit bull. Cerberus snarled as he sensed the approach of the duo. His short, matted hair was as black as coal, and the lower jowls on all three heads protruded from the trio of growling faces. The excessive underbite of each head made their lower fangs especially visible. Each razor-sharp fang was no less than six inches long. Frothing drool seeped from the trio of Cerberus' collective mouths, leaving steaming puddles of repulsive-smelling liquid spit on the ground. The eyes from all three heads glowed an unusual deep red with no distinct irises or whites.

The women approached the bizarre canine indifferently, unfazed by multi-toothed behemoth that writhed and snarled before them. Ms. Creante and Ms. Chevious stopped just in front of the three-headed creature, exchanged a shrewd smile, and joined hands. Upon contact, energy began to emanate from their bodies. They began to glow as power grew from inside them. The air around them crackled with electricity.

Suddenly, a massive blast of concussive energy shot out from the enjoined hands of the deadly duo. The blast sliced through the air like a bolt of lightning, striking Cerberus with tremendous force.

Cerberus exploded into millions of smaller dogs. The newly formed dogs ran off into countless different directions. Within seconds, the doorway that had once been occupied by the legendary three-headed dog was now empty, replaced only by the echoes of distant barks and growls as the Hounds ran off to begin the hunt.

The two women smiled. They had released the Hounds to seek out the Gift. The ladies unclasped their hands, turned, and reentered the waiting elevator.

"Take her up please, Roger," requested Ms. Creante. "Yes, ma'am," Roger said.

6

THE LOW-RIDER

Makenna sat in Mr. Rose's social studies class. She heard his voice, but his words went in one ear and out the other. Her mind was racing, her stomach nauseous. The last twelve hours had been all too much for her. Heather Stern and the Science Fair just didn't seem all that important anymore.

Why me? I can't do this. I told them I was no warrior. I'm a kid. Why didn't it matter to them?

Makenna's thoughts were interrupted by the sound of her own name being called out.

"Makenna! Makenna Gold!" Mr. Rose said sharply. "I've called on you three times and you haven't answered me."

Heather let a slight giggle escape. Mr. Rose ignored it.

"Sorry, Mr. Rose," Makenna answered, feeling herself blush. "I'm just tired. My Mom went to the hospital to have her babies this morning and... well, I'm sorry."

"I understand, and please accept my congratulations," answered Mr. Rose with congenial smile.

He directed his attention to the rest of the class. It was obvious that he sensed Makenna's embarrassment, and he didn't want to make it worse.

"Now class," he continued, "we were talking about the fight between David and Goliath. David was the youngest of eight sons. Goliath was rumored to have stood over nine feet tall. Every morning for forty days, Goliath challenged the Israelites, asking for someone to come out and fight him, but none would go. David convinced the king of the Israelites that he could defeat Goliath, even though he was a mere child and a shepherd boy at that, not at all a trained warrior."

When Makenna heard the words 'a mere child', her ears perked up, and she became very interested in the lesson.

"David was considered too young for the king's army," Mr. Rose continued, "and he even turned down an offer of the king's own armor because it was too big for him. As the story goes, David fought and killed Goliath with a single, perfectly accurate shot from his sling, perhaps with a little help from an angel. The stone didn't just rebound off the giant's skull but actually penetrated it with the power of a bullet."

It wasn't an angel. It was probably a very stubborn fairy, she thought, remembering how both Bree and Dee held her up, despite their tiny size.

"What is interesting to note about this story," Mr. Rose said, "is that David defeated a brutal giant with nothing more than a sling. Not a sword, not a spear, but a simple sling. David was a shepherd and had used the sling throughout his life to protect his flock of sheep from wild animals. For David, the sling was a part of him, as lethal in his hands as any bow or spear would be in the hands of the most brutal warrior. I feel that part of the moral of the story is that through our lives we develop our gifts, our talents, our weapons if you will. They are a part of us. Ultimately, our greatest weapons come from within. It is up to us to develop them and use them wisely."

Makenna was mesmerized by the lesson. She felt a deep sense of familiarity. It was as if Mr. Rose was talking to her directly, describing it as she was living it.

She had heard the story before, but now it meant so much more. The story of the young shepherd boy gave her hope. Hope was something she desperately needed right now. If David, a child much like her, could overcome a giant when an entire army couldn't, maybe, just maybe, she could protect her family after all.

Makenna was once again lost in thought, until the sound of the lunch bell startled her. The other students began to pack up their things.

Mr. Rose managed to yell out over the noise, "Three paragraphs by Friday on what the story means to you. Enjoy your lunch, everyone."

Mr. Rose's instructions were met by sighs and grumbles, as the students reacted to the homework assignment. As her classmates filed out of the room, Makenna stayed behind.

She approached her teacher. "Mr. Rose? May I ask you something?" "Certainly Makenna, that's why I'm here," he said with a smile.

"Do you really believe what you said about the story? You know, about developing our gifts?"

"Not only do I believe it, I live by it. Look at you, Makenna. Your sensitivity, your thoughtfulness to others, these are very powerful gifts."

Makenna smiled, though she couldn't help thinking those gifts weren't going to be much help in battling the forces of evil.

Mr. Rose laid a gentle hand on her shoulder. "You'll soon discover that these gifts will soften even the hardest heart, and win you rewards you never even anticipated. Now, go enjoy your lunch, and congratulations again on being a new big sister."

"Thank you, Mr. Rose." Makenna felt warmed by his compliments, though she wasn't quite convinced that her gifts were truly as useful as a well-placed slingshot to the head.

THE SCIENCE FAIR came and went. Heather's ice cream-maker won first place. Makenna took second for her crystallization project, but she didn't even mind. She had more pressing concerns, and even as Heather gloated while accepting her first place ribbon, all Makenna could think about was going back to the hospital to hold her new brother and sister. She got excited just thinking about it.

Makenna waited at the school drop-off/pick-up point, watching the other kids playing in the yard.

If only they knew, she thought. *Who would have believed things like defenders of hope, even fairies, were all real.*

————————

MAKENNA'S entire perception of reality had changed in less than a day. She saw her father's car pull into the school drive. She grabbed her book bag and began to run to the car, but her father opened the door and got out. His smile stretched from ear to ear, and it looked like he had something behind his back. He looked like the cat that swallowed the canary.

"Hi Dad," she called, "Are we going to the hospital?"

"Just as soon as you open this." Her father revealed what he was attempting to hide behind his thin five-foot-eleven frame. Makenna had a pretty good idea what it was, even though it was clumsily wrapped.

"Let me guess: you wrapped it yourself?" she teased.

"Not one of my talents, I know," he answered sheepishly, his grey blue eyes highlighted by his blushing cheeks.

"Oh, you know I don't care about the wrapping!" Makenna laughed. "I've wanted my own Low-rider for so long!"

Low-riders were the newest innovation in skateboarding technology - a combination skateboard/rollerblade. It looked like a typical skateboard, but with a completely new and original wheel configuration that allowed the rider to execute sharper turns and move from side to side at much greater speeds. The Low-rider acquired its name because the flexible rubber spine gave the rider the ability to bounce up and down on the board, which mimicked the motion created by hydraulics in low-rider automobiles.

Makenna had learned to use the Low-rider by borrowing her friend Bridgit's. Bridgit hardly ever used the thing, and Makenna became extremely proficient at riding it. Bridgit had offered it to her, but

Makenna refused the generous offer because she thought it would be rude. Now, though, she had her own Low-rider and she was very happy.

"Thanks Dad, I love it!" Makenna exclaimed. "What's the occasion?"
"Don't ask me," he answered, "ask Emi and Noah, it's a present

from them."

"Dad, come on." Her eyebrows raised. "Really?"

"I'm serious! They told me you deserved it. Now let's get going so we don't keep them waiting."

As they drove to the hospital, she unwrapped her new Low-rider board and admired it. It was all shiny and fresh, not a scratch on it. It almost seemed a shame to use it, but she still couldn't wait to try it out.

"We're here, baby," Dad announced. "Let's go see that new brother and sister of yours."

Makenna followed her father through the hospital parking lot, clutching her new Low-rider, which she couldn't bear to leave in the car. Her father seemed very excited because he was practically running.

"Dad, wait up," she called.

Her father stopped and turned around, still smiling. "Sorry baby," he panted, "it's just that I ..."

Suddenly, Makenna heard the screech of tires from the parking lot entrance. She turned and saw a car round the bend and rush straight for her father. The driver beeped his horn but made no move to slow down. Her father froze where he stood, like a deer caught in headlights. Makenna watched in horror as the scene seemed to play out in slow motion.

Without a thought, Makenna dropped the Low-rider onto the pavement. She hopped on the board and pushed off in her father's direction. The board shot forward with remarkable speed, closing the distance in an instant. She held out her right arm and knocked him off his feet as she careened by. The momentum sent them both flying out of the way of the oncoming car. Father and daughter landed in a soft flowerbed. The car roared past them without slowing down, continuing to honk as it turned the corner and sped out of the parking lot.

Cushioned by the soft soil of the flowerbed, Makenna's father landed first on his back, followed by Makenna and her Low-rider board to his right.

"Dad, are you okay?" she asked, practically breathless.

"I'm fine, baby. How 'bout you, are you okay?" he responded, sounding dazed.

"I'm fine. But that car was headed straight for you!"

"I know!" he said "He was driving like a bat out of... well, never mind. Thank you, baby. If not for you and that Low-rider, I'd be a resident of this hospital, not a visitor. You're pretty good on that thing. You were practically flying!"

Tears welled up in her eyes. "I love you, Dad."

He leaned over and kissed her cheek. "I love you too, sweetie. Now, let's get going. I think we've had enough excitement for one day."

"No kidding!" Makenna stood up and brushed the dust from her clothes.

"Don't forget your Low-rider!" he reminded her.

Forget it? she thought. *I may sleep with it from now on!*

7

THE FRIEND

Makenna sat out in the hospital courtyard finishing her French fries. "Is every day going to be like this?" she wondered.

It was bad enough that she had to deal with all this new responsibility, but before she'd even had time to process it, she had to save her Dad's life. This was all too much for one day.

"Hey kid!" said a voice.

Where did that come from?

The voice didn't sound anything like the fairies she'd met; it was low and gravelly. Makenna looked around, but there was no one there.

"Hey kid, down here!" the voice called.

Makenna looked down. There, in the potted plant next to her table, was an earthworm rooting around in the soil. It seemed to be looking at her.

"Yes, me!" exclaimed the worm. "You were just looking at me, kid. I'm down here in the plant. You can't miss me, long, pink, naturally segmented body."

Makenna gaped in disbelief. As if she hadn't dealt with enough in the last twenty-four hours... now an earthworm was trying to engage her in conversation!

"I don't believe this. A worm? Seriously? What's next?" she muttered. "What's wrong kid, you too good for the soil set?" the worm retorted. "You didn't look so high and mighty when you were lying in the

flowerbed a couple of hours ago. By the way, nice job back there." "You saw that?" she asked. Are you... I mean, who are you?" "I'm your assignment. Or you're mine."

Her brow furrowed. "What do you mean?"

"C'mon kid! The big guy, you know, the man upstairs, he asked me to help you out in any way I can. And since I get very valuable information down here ...well, you know."

"Know what?" she asked. "Now I'm even more confused!"

"C'mon kid, help me out here," he said. "I'm your backup. Like a spy. I hear everything that goes on down here. I'm part of the underground. Underground, get it?"

She suppressed an eye-roll. If he'd had eyebrows, he'd probably be waggling them at his own joke. "How do I know I can trust you?" she asked, skeptical. "Marigold said to be careful who I trust."

"Look, kid, the expression is a snake in the grass, not a worm in the soil."

In some weird way, and considering all that she had already been through, this made sense to Makenna.

"Oh, okay, good," she said, disappointment evident in her voice."

Harry Potter gets an owl, and I get a worm, Makenna thought, wondering how long she had to stay, to be polite.

"Listen kid, you'll pardon the pun," said the worm, "but don't sell us short. You surface walkers are the newcomers. We've been digging through this planet for 120 million years, and we're pretty smart too. After all, the expression 'bookworm' didn't come from nothing."

"I never thought of that." Against all odds, this bizarre conversation was beginning to feel more normal. "I'm sorry if I hurt your feelings," she added apologetically.

"It's okay kid," he answered. "I can get a little sensitive. I mean, I do have five hearts, so it's pretty easy to bruise one of them."

She smiled. "Do you have a name?"

"Actually, I don't," he replied. "I mean, I do among the gang down here, but you probably couldn't pronounce it. The only way to say my actual name is by shooting a mucus ball through your throat while simultaneously coughing."

"Uhm... eww," she said quickly, cutting off any further explanation. "Okay, how about I just give you a name I can pronounce."

"Oh boy, here we go," said the worm with more than a little sarcasm. "Let me guess: Slimy? Wormy? Pinky? Please, kid, not Pinky. Anything but Pinky."

Makenna racked her brain, rifling through the myriad of possibilities.

After a few moments, it hit her. "How about Fluffy?" "*Fluffy?*" he echoed.

"Yeah, Fluffy," she said. "That was the name of my favorite stuffed animal when I was growing up. If I must have a worm as a friend, he may as well have a really cute name."

He seemed to consider this. "All right, Fluffy it is."

"So, are you from around here, Fluffy? You have a little bit of an accent," Makenna said with as much politeness as possible.

He drew himself up in pride. "Oh, it's from back East. I picked it up when I spent a few years in the Big Apple. You know... New York City? I like spending time in any apple, if ya catch my meaning."

"Funny," she said with a slight groan. "Do all worms have such a corny sense of humor?"

"Lighten up kid, it's a joke."

"I know," she answered. "It's probably just my mood. I mean, this is all happening so fast. It's a lot for me to take. This Virago stuff and protecting the babies and someone trying to run over my Dad today and... I just don't think I can do this."

"Are you kidding me! You did great," Fluffy said encouragingly. "The way you just reacted back there! Do you really think anyone is trained or prepared for this? You were chosen for a reason, and based on what I saw I know why. By the way, I don't think that little car event was planned."

"What do you mean?"

"I mean, the latest word from down under is that the Evil One doesn't know where you guys are. I heard he just released the Hounds to search you out."

"The Hounds?"

"Hounds are scout dogs. There are literally millions of them. They roam the planet, looking for, well, I guess ...you. Not exactly the nicest puppies if you run into them."

"Great, more good news," Makenna said, sounding despondent. "Don't worry, kid, it could be years before they find you," Fluffy said.

"Because the Hounds are still roaming, I don't think that little car stunt was intentional."

"What was it then?"

"Don't ask me. Could be nothing more than some crazy driver. Could be coincidental. Coincidences do happen, you know."

Makenna shrugged. "I suppose so."

"Good," Fluffy said. "Look kid, I gotta go, the rose bushes in the flower bed lost some leaves when you guys fell on them, and they look delicious. I want to get to them before the rest of the gang does. I'll catch up wit yas later."

"Goodbye, Fluffy. It was really nice meeting you." "Nice talking to you too," he answered.

"What's wrong?" Makenna asked.

She had noticed a strange expression on his face. The fact that she noticed any expression in his worm face at all was a little weird.

"Well..." he answered, "it's just nobody has ever said it was nice meeting me before. I guess it made me a little emotional. It's these five hearts, I tell ya. Never know when one of them is gonna kick in. You're a nice kid. You be careful. Okay?"

As Makenna nodded in agreement, she heard her father calling her name. "Over here, Dad!"

"What are you doing out here, Makenna?" her father asked, walking toward her. "Mom's been asking for you."

"Gotta go, Fluffy," she whispered. Then she blew him a kiss and was gone.

"It looked like you were talking to those plants," Dad said. "Dad, don't be silly." She faked a laugh.

THE EARTHWORM WATCHED as Makenna and her father went back inside the hospital.

She's a good one, he thought. *This whole Virago thing on a nice kid like that... wow, what was the big guy thinking?*

With that thought, the worm melted back into the dirt.

8

THE NANNY

Several days passed without incident. No speeding cars trying to run her father down, no fairy appearances. Other than the occasional visit from Fluffy while out playing in the backyard, Makenna almost forgot that she was the Virago, or anything but a normal twelve-year-old girl.

Makenna was beyond impressed that Fluffy was able to make his way from the hospital where they met to her own backyard, and she did enjoy his sarcastic sense of humor... most of the time.

Her mom and the babies had been home for over a week, and as much as it was an adjustment, she loved having her siblings home. She didn't mind the crying at night and having to be quiet during the day. They were so sweet and tiny. It was all worth it.

When Emi and Noah were sleeping, Makenna would go outside and practice on her new Low-rider board. She soon mastered full 360's, uphill acceleration, and airborne spins. Her father even took her to the local skateboard park to practice on the ramps. He got her all new protective gear including helmet, kneepads, and elbow pads. Makenna made sure she wore it whenever she was Low-riding. Not only did it protect her, but it made her feel like she looked fierce, especially the helmet, which was a light blue shade with cloud designs. The more she rode, the more she real-

ized that her Low-rider felt different from Bridgit's. She could swear that sometimes she was skating on a cushion of air. On occasion, when she looked down at her board it seemed to be glowing, as if electricity was running through it.

Makenna was determined to be the best Low-rider in California. She was already better than most of the other kids with regular skate- boards, even on the ramps. Boy, if Heather could see her now!

She was practicing double rear wheel 360's in front of the house when she heard her Dad call for her. "Makenna, can you come in? We have company coming. I want you to clean up."

"Coming, Dad," she answered.

Who is coming over? she wondered.

It was kind of weird. Practically the entire family had already been by to see the twins, and she didn't remember hearing anything about a visit today.

Makenna walked into the house, removed her gear, and went to the bathroom to wash up. As she turned on the faucet, the doorbell rang. Her father bolted for the door to prevent the visitor from ringing again. Mother and the twins were all napping, and he didn't want them waking up.

"Hello, Mr. Gold," said an unfamiliar voice.

Makenna glanced up as she continued to soap up her hands and face.

It was someone with an accent.

"It is so nice to meet you," the visitor added. "I'm Lucy Revel." "Pleasure, Ms. Revel. Come on in and have a seat in the living room,"

Dad said. "Forgive me, I'm a little out of breath. My wife is taking a nap while the babies are down for their naps. I didn't want the doorbell to wake them up."

"No need to apologize," the woman said cheerfully. "That's quite a handful you've got; three children and two new babies. No worries though, I cared for a family of five children ranging in all ages back in Londonderry."

Makenna turned off the water and stood quietly, just listening.

"Well that's perfect, my wife and I could certainly use the help around here," Dad answered. "Our oldest daughter, Makenna, is twelve. She's quite the helper herself."

"Makenna... now that is a beautiful name."

"Thank you. My wife was inspired by a character from the movie *Somewhere in Time*. The babies' names are Emilyne and Noah."

"Sweet names for sweet angels," Ms. Revel said.

"Speaking of which..." Dad began to look around for his eldest daughter. "Makenna? Why don't you come out here and meet Ms. Revel?"

Makenna left the bathroom and stepped warily into the living room. *What is a Ms. Revel?* she wondered.

When Makenna caught sight of the visitor, she thought the woman couldn't look less like the word "revel" if she tried. She had jet black hair tied back so tightly it looked like her skin was being stretched across her face, barely covering her bones. Her narrow, hooked nose accentuated this. Her face was extremely thin, her cheeks sunken. Her eyes bulged out, but her eye sockets were very dark, making her look simultaneously overenergized and exhausted.

"Oh, there you are, Makenna." Her father sounded pleased. "This is Ms. Revel. We may be hiring her to help us out over the next few months."

"But Dad!" Makenna said anxiously, "you said I would be helping you and Mom. I mean we..."

"Of course, baby," he assured her. "You're already a huge help. But you can't always be here. What about school and your friends?"

Ms. Revel fixed Makenna with an alarmingly wide smile. She had thin pale lips, and her forced smile revealed long skinny teeth that looked too big for her mouth.

"Not to worry, love," Ms. Revel said, still smiling her awful smile. "We're all going to get along famously, and I'm sure I'm going to need your help as well. After all, there's lots for me to learn around here."

Makenna thoroughly disliked her already. In addition to her resembling a rodent, there was something phony about her. And that accent, like a cheap knockoff of Mary Poppins. And why was she talking down to Makenna, treating her like a small child? Makenna knew when someone

was being, what did Mr. Rose call it again? *Condescending. That's what she is,* Makenna thought. Nonetheless, Makenna attempted to hide her feelings, without much success.

"Makenna what's wrong?" her father asked. "Ms. Revel just said she'd need your help."

Makenna had been so caught up in staring at Ms. Revel's rodent-like face, she had forgotten to say anything at all. "Ohh! Yeah, sorry, Dad ... I'd be happy to help Ms. Revel," she answered, stumbling over her words.

"Oh, she's a doll, that one is," Ms. Revel said.

Dad can't be falling for this woman's phony act. Can he? Maybe he's just being polite.

"Well, your references and experience are impeccable, Ms. Revel. When can you start?"

Makenna tried to stifle a gasp. *NO! How could he even consider hiring this woman?*

"Makenna, are you okay?" her father asked, puzzled by her reaction. "Yeah Dad ... uh... I'm fine," She tried to hide her disbelief. "I just

have to go outside and... I think I left something out there."

"Okay sweetie, but don't be too long," he said, returning his attention to the new nanny. "Now Ms. Revel, why don't I show you around?"

"Please call me Lucy," she said.

Makenna winced at the woman's sickly-sweet tone as she closed the door behind her and sprinted to the backyard.

Makenna felt sick to her stomach. Something was very wrong with all of this. She got down on all fours frantically sifting through the grass.

"Fluffy? Fluffy, it's me. Fluffy, where are you?"

Fluffy popped his head up through the soil. "Calm down, I hear you," he said, sounding irritated. "I was just munchin' on some sunflower roots. What's wrong?"

"Are you sure that bad guy, the evil one, whatever his name is, doesn't know where we are?" she asked.

"As far as I know, yeah," he answered, "Why?"

"It's this new nanny my Dad just hired," Makenna said. "Her name's Ms. Revel. Something about her isn't right."

"Look kid, I can only tell you what I hear about down here, and I usually hear it all. I mean after all, it is the underground," Fluffy said. "Far as I know, the Hounds are still out looking for you."

"These Hounds, what exactly are they?" Makenna asked.

"Just what I said, Hounds. Very nasty canines, trained to sniff out and track the scent of good or hope. The babies emit this essence in spades. It's called Efflusyum. You ever notice how just being around the twins makes you feel good?"

"Yeah, but I just thought it was because they were so cute."

"Well that's part of it, but there's more," Fluffy explained. "Emi and Noah emit an aura of good. If the Hounds catch that scent, they'll come runnin."

"And you're sure they're dogs, not rats, huh?"

"Look, kid, it's possible they're taking a rodent form this time," said the worm. "But in the past, they've always been dogs; big, ugly, mean, I'm-gonna-bite-your-face-off dogs."

"Still, I'm gonna keep my eye on that woman," Makenna said. "I don't like her one bit."

He shrugged his little wormy... shoulders? "Well, I'll listen around down here and see if I pick up anything new. Now can I get back to my roots?"

"Yes. Thanks, Fluffy." She made a move to go back into the house. "Oops! I almost forgot." She turned back to the earthworm and blew him a kiss

"Thanks, kid!" he said, his pink body turning a little pinker.

Makenna went back inside. The babies were awake lying in their bassinets. Makenna's mother was going through some of the daily chores and routines with Ms. Revel.

"Hi baby, were you outside playing?" Mom asked. "Yes, Mom. How was your nap?"

"Great, thank you baby. Have you met Ms. Revel?"

"Oh yes, we have met, and young Miss Makenna has already promised to be my helper," Ms. Revel interjected.

How rude! Mom was asking me, thought Makenna.

"Makenna really is a great helper Ms. Revel," Mom said, brightly. "The babies love her already. The minute she picks them up, they stop crying. I think they think Makenna is their mother."

"Moooooom," Makenna drawled, blushing.

"Ms. Revel, if you wish you can begin to move your things into the guest bedroom," Mom said.

"Move in?" Makenna repeated in disbelief. "She's moving into our house?" She glared at Ms. Revel, even more convinced this woman was an impostor. Had she cast some kind of spell over her parents? Was she after the babies? "Mom, I swear I can help with the babies. I promise I'll do whatever you need."

"I know you will, Ken," her Mother answered with softness in her voice. "Ms. Revel will be here as a backup when you aren't here."

"Don't you worry, poppet, Ms. Revel will only be here to help madam with those two little angels," the woman said, referring to herself in the third person.

"Makenna, you look awfully pale," her mother said. "I'm just very tired," Makenna assured her.

"Do you have a fever, sweetie?" her mother asked, pressing a hand to Makenna's forehead.

"A bit of tea might do her well, ma'am," Ms. Revel said. "I'll just pop into the kitchen and put the kettle on."

"I don't want any tea!" Makenna exclaimed.

"Makenna Grace Gold!" her mother admonished. "Ms. Revel was only trying to help."

At her mother's biting words, Makenna felt her temper cool. "Sorry Mom, sorry Ms. Revel."

"Ohh, pish posh ma'am, the little one doesn't feel well – it's understandable."

"Thank you for your understanding, Ms. Revel, but Makenna knows better."

THAT EVENING, after the twins had finally been cajoled into sleep, Makenna lay in bed. Her face brightened as her mother walked into the room.

"Honey, I know you have a problem with Ms. Revel being here," she said. "And I know you want to help, and you will. I promise. Trust me. Your brother and sister are crazy about you. I know she may come off a little strange at first, but let's give the nanny a chance, okay?"

"I'll try," Makenna said. She didn't want her mother worrying.

"Try to get some sleep. I love you very much." She bent down to kiss Makenna goodnight.

"I love you too," Makenna said, returning the kiss on her mother's cheek. Her mother turned the light off and left the room.

Makenna began to feel a little better. Her mother had admitted that Ms. Revel was a little strange. She had not completely fooled Mom. Now, Makenna had to make sure the Nanny didn't get away with anything else. Tomorrow was Saturday, and Makenna was determined to stick to Lucy Revel like glue.

9

THE HOUND

The sun shone through the blinds so brightly it woke Makenna out of a restless sleep.

Makenna nestled under the covers, hoping to doze a little longer. Then came that phony Mary Poppins voice.

"The weather is so beautiful. Why don't I take the little ones to the park in their carriage?"

Makenna's heart jumped in her chest, and she leapt out of bed

"The park? With all that sunlight? The babies aren't even two weeks old," Makenna's mother said.

Way to go Mom, thought Makenna, scrambling to get her clothes on.

Don't you let those babies out of the house!

"Not to worry. They need fresh air, and little sunlight helps prevent jaundice," the Nanny explained.

"That makes sense. Okay, maybe just for a half hour or so."

Makenna grabbed her Low-rider and flew out of her room. Ms. Revel already had the baby carriage out and the diaper bag slung over her shoulder.

"I'm going with you," Makenna declared.

An odd expression flashed across the Nanny's face, replaced almost instantly with a sickening smile.

"My, my, young lady, aren't we a different little missy this morning," Ms. Revel said. "Feeling better, are we?"

"I'm sorry about last night, Ms. Revel. I was just tired, but I'd love to come with you to the park and practice my Low-rider," Makenna said with a matching fake smile of her own.

Makenna had decided to play Ms. Revel's game. If Ms. Revel could play Mary Poppins, Makenna could play Pollyanna, full of exaggerated sweetness. "What a wonderful idea!" Makenna's mother exclaimed with delight.

"You and Ms. Revel will have a wonderful time."

Once outside, Makenna skated in large circles around the Nanny as Ms. Revel pushed the babies in their carriage.

"You're good on that thing, poppet," Ms. Revel observed.

Makenna didn't respond. She twisted her hips and masterfully performed a rear wheel 360, holding her head up high and feeling like she was dancing on air. She wasn't going to be lulled into a false sense of secu- rity by a random compliment.

"Ms. Revel, may I ask you a question?" Makenna sailed past the Nanny in another elegant loop.

"Certainly, poppet."

"Why are you really here?"

Ms. Revel's eyes narrowed slightly, but the smile remained on her lips. "To help your family, love. After all, new babies are a lot of work."

"No really, why are you here?" Makenna asked. "I don't understand your question."

"I think you do," Makenna murmured, just softly enough to avoid being heard. She was not likely to get anywhere with this line of question- ing, so she continued riding on her board until they made it to the park.

As they walked through the park entrance, Makenna sailed ahead, enjoying the cool breeze through her hair. Ms. Revel sat down on a park bench, the stroller just in front of her. The babies were close by under Makenna's watchful eye and for the moment, Makenna didn't have a care in the world. That brief respite was, however, about to come to a crashing end.

The cool breeze suddenly disappeared, as if something had literally sucked the air out of the atmosphere.

Makenna noticed the change instantly. Almost on instinct, Makenna felt her stomach knot up. She spun the board around, facing the bench where Ms. Revel sat with the baby carriage. Ms. Revel seemed to be oblivious to the vacuum effect Makenna was experiencing.

Makenna pushed off in the direction of the bench, scanning the park for anything unusual. A large black canine sniffing the pathway drew her attention. The dog was huge, with a thick broad chest. The lower half of his jaw jutted out from his square head. His lower fangs were clearly visi- ble. The animal meandered along the pathway with his nose to the pavement.

Suddenly, the black beast snapped its head up, like a hungry wolf who had caught the scent of its unwitting prey. At that moment, the canine unexpectedly turned his square head toward her and looked directly at her. She froze as the beast stared her down, its eyes resembling two glowing red orbs. It was obvious that creature was not of this earth. This had to be one of the infamous Hounds she had been warned about. Emi and Noah were in danger. She had to get them out of there!

As if on cue, the twins began to cry, maybe sensing the danger themselves. The sound of the wailing echoed through the park. The Hound heard it too, turning its massive head toward them while blowing a puff of smoke from its flared snout.

With a speed that belied its size, the beast lunged forward, making a beeline for the baby carriage, moving with the speed of an attacking viper. Her adrenaline pumping, Makenna instinctively pushed off on her board, which shot forward with astonishing speed. When she careened from the pathway to the grass, the board didn't slow down at all. Makenna glanced down long enough to register that she wasn't skating on the grass.

She was flying over it, hovering in mid-air. At that moment, Makenna had no time to even consider the fact that she was flying on her Low-Rider.

Acting on instinct alone, Makenna pointed her board directly at the dog, then slammed herself full force into its immense rib cage, attempting to knock it off course and draw its attention. The impact felt as if she had charged headlong into a solid brick wall. The collision knocked the dog into the air and sent Makenna flipping head over heels off the board and into the grass.

Makenna sat up quickly, trying to catch her breath. She realized with dismay that the Hound had recovered even faster than her. Back on all fours, the furious beast lunged toward Makenna, mounting its counter attack. With two massive leaps, the beast was on her. Makenna was barely able to get off the ground before the creature had her pinned down. Makenna attempted to sit up fully, but to no avail, as the demon Hound loomed over her.

Her face was mere inches away from the Hound's dripping fangs. Makenna could feel his acrid hot breath on her cheeks. The dog bared its teeth, letting out a menacing low snarl.

She braced herself for the attack, but the creature just stared into her eyes, taking his measure of her. The Hound seemed to delight in the intoxicating smell of Makenna's fear. The young girl went catatonic as sheer terror immobilized her. She opened her mouth to scream, but she couldn't. Literally no sound came out. She tried to move, but her muscles refused to respond.

"Get up child, fight him!" Ms. Revel shouted from the sidelines. "Fight your fear, Virago."

As if in response to Ms. Revel's pleadings, the air was pierced by Emi and Noah's cries.

The twins! she thought. The sound stirred something within her. Without any explanation, white-hot anger boiled in her veins. Instantly, fear gave way to utter rage.

"NO!" Makenna screamed. "YOU CAN'T HAVE THEM!"

She grabbed her board and smashed it into the Hound's gaping maw with every ounce of strength she could muster. Even the creature was taken off-guard as it recoiled, giving Makenna all the break she needed.

She leapt to her feet and jumped onto the Low-rider, skating away from the enraged animal.

This isn't over, Makenna realized. *I must stop that thing for good.*

Where's a good dog catcher around when you need one!

She circled back to mount a second assault. This time it would be a frontal attack. The element of surprise was gone. The Hound was ready. Makenna, now, was also ready.

The Hound primed himself, planting all fours firmly in place, fixing his ominous gaze on Makenna. His eyes glowed even brighter, turning from red to white hot. Without warning, two bolts of fire shot out from the Hounds' eyes, like dual laser beams.

"The board, Virago, use the board!" It was Ms. Revel again. Makenna barely had time to register the fact that Ms. Revel was not only helping her from the sidelines but referring to her as the Virago.

Makenna pressed her weight down on the rear of the board, sending the Low-rider board soaring while dodging the oncoming bolts of fire. The bolts missed Makenna and hit a tree behind her. The tree was instantly engulfed in flame, sending the other people in the park into a panic as it lit up like a huge Roman Candle. People ran in all directions as panic ensued.

Where is Ms. Revel? Where are the babies?

Makenna felt something slam into her head, vibrating through her helmet. As she looked around to see what hit her, she spotted two more bolts flying off into the air. The daggers of fire spawned from the Hounds' eyes seemed to have ricocheted off her helmet.

This gave Makenna an idea. She maneuvered her board up and swooped around, circling around the dog and approaching from the rear to make herself a more difficult target.

The animal spun around to face her with gloating eyes, as if sensing that it had already won. The red orbs again began to glow, preparing to unleash another burst.

Makenna jumped off her board and grabbed it with both hands, holding it out in front of her body as a makeshift shield. She felt the impact of the fire bolts as it hit the board, the impact forcing her to stagger back.

The fire bolts rebounded off the board and sped directly back at the evil creature. The instant the bolts made contact, the animal vaporized in a puff of black smoke, leaving only the foul smell of burnt hair and charred dog behind.

Live by fire, die by the fire, she thought triumphantly. Her idea had worked.

Her joy was short lived as she began choking and coughing on the pungent smoke left behind by the vaporized Hound. She rubbed her eyes, which were stinging from the overpowering smell.

"Nice work, Virago," came a voice from behind her. Makenna spun around, raising her board like a weapon. "Defender, HOLD!"

She froze. It was Ms. Revel. Makenna still did not trust the Nanny, but her stomach was no longer tight with fear. Something inside her told her that the danger has passed. Furthermore, Makenna could see the babies were no longer agitated, but instead resting quietly in their carriage next to Ms. Revel.

"Everything is all right. It's me, Marigold," said the Nanny. "Marigold?" Makenna asked, dumbfounded.

"Yes child, it's me," the Nanny repeated calmly. She put her hands on Makenna's shoulders. "Ms. Revel is my human form, my cover, if you will."

Tears pricked at Makenna's eyes. "But how ...why...?"

"I was charged with your training, child," she answered. "I turned myself into Ms. Revel so that I could be close to you and the twins."

"But then why didn't you tell me? Why did you bring the twins here? That... that... *thing* almost killed me!"

"Calm down child," the Nanny said. "I was helping you. I got the twins out of harm's way, enabling you to do what you had to do to defeat the creature. To be effective at protecting the twins, you must learn how to trust your instincts. By trusting what you know, you will learn how to control your fear. If I step in for you and intervene every time there is trouble, you learn nothing. If you don't master your skills and gifts now, your future and our world will be over."

Makenna collapsed into the Nanny's arms and wept with relief.

Relief that the battle was over, relief that her brother and sister were safe, and relief that Ms. Revel was an ally, not an enemy.

Ms. Revel held Makenna and hugged her tightly, allowing her a much-needed release.

"It's okay. Let it out." The Nanny held the Virago in her arms, rubbing circles on her back.

"Thank you, Ms. Revel. I mean, Marigold," Makenna said, sniffling through her tears.

"You were wonderful, child," she replied. "Smart, resourceful, and you adapted quickly. I am so proud of you. Noah and Emi couldn't be in better hands. The Enlightened one again has chosen wisely." She released Makenna and flashed a smile. "Now let's go home. I don't know about you, but I'm famished! Even a fairy needs her sustenance."

10

THE ARMASWORD

Ms. Revel sat in her room, reviewing the day's battle in her head. The twins had just gone down for the evening, and Makenna's Mom and Dad were in the den watching a movie. It was the perfect quiet time for reflection. Bree and Dee were buzzing eagerly around her room.

"We watched her today," said Bree, "she did a wonderful job."

"I know, Bree," Ms. Revel replied. "I was proud of her as well, defeating a Hound on her first battle, very impressive. Her predecessors at least had a chance to work up to that. My concern is that these Hounds found us too quickly. We shouldn't have encountered them for months. Something's wrong. Someone must have tipped them off."

"But who, Marigold?" asked Bree.

"I'll bet it's that darned social media," said Dee with conviction. There was a knock at the door. Bree and Dee flew behind the vanity.

"Ms. Revel, it's Makenna, may I come in?" "Certainly child," answered the Nanny.

Makenna entered, closing the door quietly behind her. "You can come out now, ladies," the Nanny said drolly.

"Whew!" sighed Dee Delphine in relief. "We thought it might have been the Mister or Missus," She flew out from behind the vanity, followed by her cousin.

"Excellent job today, ma'am," said Bree, buzzing excitedly around the room. "We watched you fly. You're a natural."

"Thank you, Bree." Makenna blushed at the compliment. "I was gonna ask you about that, Marigold."

"Oh, you mean your Low-rider?" asked the Nanny. "Let me explain, poppet. When you bonded with the sword, traditionally known as the Arma or Armasword, you were given the ultimate weapon. That weapon became a part of you. Like your hand or leg, it is now literally an extension of your body, the ultimate expression of your power and your soul. As the bearer of the Armasword, you may determine the form of the weapon. Past Defenders have chosen the weapon that they felt most comfortable using. It would seem that either consciously or unconsciously, you have chosen to use the Low-rider board as your weapon of choice.

"Along with its form," she continued, "the Armasword has been infused with a few, shall we say, *extra* powers. It is virtually indestructible, along with your protective gear."

"Oh, so that's why it made such an excellent shield!" said Makenna with awe.

"Yes Makenna, and as you have noticed it also has been blessed with angel wings."

"What does that mean?"

"The board can fly, my dear," said Ms. Revel, almost casually. "Yes, and you're really good at flying it," interrupted Bree.

Marigold shot a quick disapproving scowl at Bree. "It's rude to interrupt, my dear."

"Sorry ma'am," the fairy apologized.

Marigold continued, "Yes child, it seems your weapon can fly."

"I wish you guys had told me all of this before," Makenna said, sounding slightly resentful.

Marigold took a deep breath and answered. "We don't always know everything in advance, child. The path of a Defender is one of ongoing discovery and adaptation. The fact is, we can give you guidance and direction, but the path is yours to create."

"What does that mean?" asked Makenna, exasperated.

"It means, we are all learning and growing together," Marigold answered. "Evolving, which make us stronger."

"I'm still not sure I understand."

"For now, child, be proud of yourself, as we are all proud of you. You were excellent today." Marigold put an end to the conversation, as Makenna had had enough to contend with in the past twelve hours.

"I can't stop thinking about it," said Makenna. "I don't know how I'll be able to sleep."

"Ladies," Marigold summoned Bree and Dee to her side. "Proceed." In response to Marigold's request, Bree and Dee flew over Makenna's head, sprinkling Fairy dust on it. "You will sleep well now, child, and you will dream well."

"Thank you, Marigold. Thank you, Bree and Dee," Makenna said, her mouth opening with a huge yawn.

"Sleep well child, you have more than earned it," answered Bree, smiling.

Makenna left Ms. Revel's room, closing the door behind her. Her mother met her at the door. "I was just looking for you. I thought you were in bed, young lady!"

"No Mom, I had to ask Ms. Revel something." "What?" Mom asked, a little surprised.

"Oh nothing."

"Uhmm... ok," Mom said. "I thought you weren't exactly a fan of Ms. Revel's."

"No Mom, I actually think she's really nice."

Mom nodded. "Well, I'll tell you, with all the help she gave me with your brother and sister, I felt like I had some kind of guardian angel around here today."

Makenna giggled. "Well, sort of." "What?" her mother asked, baffled. Makenna yawned.

"I'm really tired. I better go to sleep. I love you, Mommy." She gave her mother a kiss before returning to her room. Soon, Makenna was asleep.

Inside Ms. Revel's room, the three fairies continued their conversation.

"Now that she has destroyed a Hound, the Evil one will be alerted," said Bree Delphine with concern.

"I'm not certain of that," answered Marigold. "I threw a quick cloaking spell over the area the minute she destroyed the beast. If no one was paying close attention, it should be masked."

"That's perfect," replied Dee. "It's too early for Makenna to have to confront the Alghanii."

"I agree," said Bree, "hopefully, one less Hound won't send up too many alerts."

"Let us pray, sisters," said Dee.

"Yes sisters, let us pray," said Marigold. "I'll admit, this Virago is impressive, but the Alghanii are formidable!"

11

THE NEW STUDENT

Makenna was able to enjoy the rest of her weekend practicing her Low-rider and playing with the babies. At school on Monday morning, Makenna sat in Mr. Rose's class and once again found herself identifying with the subject of the lesson in a whole new way.

"Now in our study of American Presidents, who said 'The only thing we have to fear is fear itself', Heather?" asked Mr. Rose.

"Franklin Roosevelt," Heather answered.

"Very good." He faced the rest of the class. "And what do you think President Roosevelt meant by that statement?"

Heather, in her typical know-it-all manner, quickly answered, "Well, America was going through a very tough period, and I think he meant it to give people hope to continue on through the challenging times."

"Excellent, Heather," Mr. Rose said, knowing full well Heather's constant need for praise and admiration. "That's true, it was a statement of inspiration. Next question: Is fear such a bad thing? Isn't it true fear keeps us cautious or in check? Was President Roosevelt simply saying, 'Don't worry, be happy'?"

Makenna put up her hand. "Yes, Makenna?"

"I think what the President was saying is that we shouldn't let fear run our lives. It's okay to be afraid, but we shouldn't let that fear paralyze us and stop us from moving forward."

Mr. Rose nodded approvingly. "Very good, Makenna. I agree whole heartedly."

"She's obviously not ruled by fear, or she would have been afraid to wear that outfit," Heather whispered to Michelle, loudly enough for Makenna to hear. Both girls giggled.

"Ladies, is there something you wish to share with the class?" "No, Mr. Rose," Heather said, facing forward with a blush.

"Then let's stop the chatter, shall we?" he said, and continued with the lesson. "Makenna's correct. It's all right to be afraid and to acknowledge our fears. Fear can serve as a tool to keep us in check. It can serve to remind us to examine or assess the situation, but we shouldn't let our fears paralyze us. We must learn to confront them and move on. Any questions?"

Makenna just smiled, thinking how she had learned this very lesson in practice over the weekend.

There was a knock at the door. Mrs. Rosenzweig, the school principal, poked her head into the classroom. "I'm sorry to interrupt, Mr. Rose, but I want to introduce a new student to the class," she said. "May I come in?"

"Certainly, Mrs. Rosenzweig," he answered, waving her in.

She stepped into the room, a nervous-looking boy behind her. "Students, I'd like to introduce a new student who has just moved here all the way from Toronto, Canada," she announced with a smile. "I'm sure you will all help him out and make him feel comfortable. This is Stephen Levine. Stephen, if you don't mind, just take that desk over there next to Makenna." She pointed to the empty desk by the window. "You can put your supplies in the desk and Mr. Rose will help you get your books."

Mr. Rose gave Stephen a reassuring smile. "Welcome to my class, Stephen. My name is Mr. Rose."

Thank you," Stephen replied, proceeding to the empty desk. He and Makenna glanced at each other at the same moment, simultaneously blushing as the class focused on the exchange.

Out of the corner of her eye, Makenna watched the new arrival as he took his seat. He looked to be a couple inches taller than her, with short, dark hair and muscular arms for a seventh-grader. She couldn't help wonder if he liked skateboarding.

Once seated, Stephen opened his bag and began to put some of his things in the desk.

"You are very fortunate, Stephen," said Mr. Rose. "Makenna will be a wonderful mentor. If there is anything I can do to make your adjustment easier, please let me know."

"Thank you, sir," the boy answered shyly.

"Before we resume, Stephen, I'd love it if you would tell us a little about yourself."

He seemed a little embarrassed, at first. He blushed and smiled, which made his dark curly hair and blue eyes stand out. "Well... okay... my name is Stephen. I'm new to California, obviously," he added, sounding slightly embittered. "My parents moved me and my brother here because they are animators and they got some big job down here. I left all my friends in Toronto, and I'm a big Maple Leafs fan."

"Okay, Stephen, thank you," Mr. Rose said.

Makenna felt bad for Stephen. It must have been awful leaving all his friends behind, then moving such a huge distance away. She promised herself that she would do all she could to help show him around and make him feel welcome. It was the right thing to do. Plus, he was cute.

She leaned over quietly and whispered, "If you want, you can sit by me at lunch in the cafeteria." He smiled briefly and nodded.

He has a nice smile, she thought.

12

THE UNITED STATES

"No, President Chen, my company is honored to assist you in your ongoing struggle with the People's Liberation Army. I will set up a meeting when you arrive in London with my R & D Strategists."

Sir Seaton sat behind his desk, running his forefinger and thumb along the outline of his raven black moustache and goatee. The multibillionaire reclined in his leather chair, listening to the response on his speakerphone.

"Yes, Mr. President," Seaton answered, "I will see you in a few days. I look forward to sharing tea. I trust you will be bringing some of your finest oolong from your own personal collection?" Sir Seaton let out a slight snigger in response to Chen's eagerly positive answer. "I will see you in a few days. Safe trip, Mr. President."

Seaton hung up the phone, chuckling to himself. "Anything to keep the conflict going, I always say. I wonder if he would have a problem knowing that I've been arming the other side for years. Idiotic, pedantic fools."

"Sir," the intercom buzzed in, interrupting Seaton during his exercise in self-aggrandizement, "I have Ms. Creante on the line from Jerusalem, and the replacement piece for your chessboard has just arrived."

"Thank-you, Mr. Xshun," answered Seaton. "I will be out momentarily. Connect Ms. Creante immediately."

Moments later, Mr. Xshun patched through the call. "Yes, Ms. Creante?"

"Sir, nothing has turned up on that Hound alert here in Jerusalem," came Ms. Creante's voice. "I was certain this was it. What better place to deliver his new Gift to the world than Jerusalem? However, it turned out to be nothing. We just located a spike in Hound activity in the United States, around Southern California, and another in Tehran. Should we go to Tehran first? We're not that far from there."

"No. You and Ms. Chevious make your way to the U.S. I have a suspicion about that spike. He seems to love that country. Probably something to do with their currency. 'In God We Trust', hah! What a joke. Remember," Seaton scowled, "when you find the Gift, destroy the Virago and bring the Gift to me. I intend to use it for myself."

"Yes sir, as you wish," she said dutifully.

"What is it they say? Godspeed!" he ordered, sarcasm evident in his tone.

As soon as he disconnected the line, the intercom buzzed again. "Yes, Mr. Xshun?"

"Sir, I know this seems odd but, your cat Savannah is meowing rather loudly, like she's ...hungry," the assistant said, sounding rather amazed.

"That is a good sign, Mr. Xshun. Savannah's hunger bodes well," answered Seaton. "She has not eaten a bite in over 1,000 years. Give her whatever she wants, Mr. Xshun."

Seaton disconnected the line and smiled wickedly. "God bless America," he said, laughing.

His laugh was so immense that the entire building at Number 66, 6th Street in London trembled.

13

THE BETRAYAL

Makenna bolted into her house, dropping her Low-rider just inside the front door. "MOM! I had the best day at school!"

"What, sweetie, what is it?" her mother walked into view, putting a finger over her mouth to remind Makenna to keep her voice down. "Ms. Revel and I just got the twins to sleep... now what happened that made this the best day?"

The front door opened, and her dad walked in.

"Hey, thanks for waiting, Makenna," he said sarcastically. To Mom he said, "I just put the car in park, didn't even have time to turn off the engine. The next thing I know, Makenna's bolting into the house. What's was all that about?"

"Sorry, Dad," Makenna said. "It's just that I wanted to tell Mom about Stephen!"

"Stephen?" her mother asked with a coy smile. "Who's Stephen?"

"He's my new friend," Makenna said excitedly. "He just moved here from Canada. He plays ice hockey and he's really nice." She grinned from ear to ear.

"Okay, okay, slow down, sweetie." Her mom put a finger to her lips, reminding her that the babies were asleep.

"Sorry Mom, I just had a really good day," Makenna continued at a slightly lower volume. "You know what else? I let him try my Low-rider, and he's pretty good."

"You let him try your skateboard?" Ms. Revel said, descending the stairs.

"Oh...hi, Ms. Revel. Yeah, he's pretty good."

"Are you really sure that was such a good idea, poppet?" Ms. Revel asked. "You're always on that thing. In a way, it has become a part of your body. It is almost like you loaned him your right arm." Ms. Revel gave Makenna a subtle yet stern look.

"Maybe you're right, Ms. Revel," Makenna replied, taking the hint.

"Oh, you know how Makenna is, Ms. Revel," her mother said. "If Makenna likes you, she'll give you the shirt off her back. Reminds me of the time that Makenna emptied out the refrigerator. Turns out she was feeding all the kids in the neighborhood because she felt they deserved a snack."

"Oh, I know what you mean, ma'am. A heart of gold that one has," Ms. Revel agreed. She turned to Makenna. "Can you come to the kitchen and help me put away a few things?"

"Okay." Makenna felt knots began to form in her stomach. Makenna followed Ms. Revel, sensing her disapproval.

"Dad and I are going to get changed," Makenna's mother said. "Don't forget. We have dinner reservations with Dad's boss, tonight."

Makenna stood at the kitchen sink next to Ms. Revel, awaiting the reprimand. She did not have to wait long.

"You must understand that your Low-rider is a very valuable and powerful resource," Ms. Revel said with quiet intensity. "Do you think King Arthur said, 'Hey Sir Galahad, try out this sword. I call it Excalibur, and it's really neat'!"

"No, Ms. Revel," she answered, crestfallen.

"Exactly! Makenna, I know how good-hearted you are. It is one of your strongest qualities, but under certain circumstances, it can also be exploited. Evil can and will use it against you. I'm asking you to remember who you are, and to be careful."

"I'm sorry, Marigo... I mean, Ms. Revel," she said, her cheeks flushed with embarrassment.

"Think nothing of it, child. No harm done for now."

"You know, speaking of valuable and powerful resources, Ms. Revel... I haven't seen Fluffy around for a few days now." Makenna hoped Ms. Revel would understand what she was talking about.

"Fluffy? Who's Fluffy?" Ms. Revel asked, puzzled.

Makenna was confused. She was certain that Ms. Revel would know who Fluffy was. Weren't they all working together?

"You know, Fluffy, the earthworm? A couple inches long, pink skin, tells really bad jokes?"

Ms. Revel looked even more bewildered. "What are you talking about, child? What earthworm?"

Uh-oh, she thought.

"The day Emi and Noah were born, I was approached by an earthworm at the hospital," Makenna explained. "He said he saw me rescue my Dad, and that he knew I was the Virago. He told me he had been sent to help me and give me inside information from the underground." Makenna pointed at the floor. "Kind of like a double agent."

The color drained from Ms. Revels' face.

"What? Is there something wrong?" Makenna asked. Something was very, very wrong.

"Follow me, child." Ms. Revel took Makenna by the wrist, hastily pulling Makenna into her room and closing the door behind them. She looked up at the ceiling and summoned her two aides.

"Bree, Dee...to me quickly!" she urged.

With a tiny *poof*, The two fairies appeared out of thin air right in front of them.

"What is it, ma'am? It sounds urgent," said Bree, her high-pitched voice even higher.

"We have a problem, ladies," Ms. Revel declared, her voice tinged with foreboding. "I know how the Hound found us so quickly."

Makenna was silent, fearing she had done something wrong again.

This felt far worse than just loaning out her Low-rider board to someone she just met.

"He used a worm!" Ms. Revel stated.

"What? Already?" Bree asked. Dee gasped in shock.

"He must have gotten the word out about the Gift quickly. The worm must have tipped a Hound to our location, ladies. And we know what that means."

"The Alghanii could well be on their way, if they're not already here, lurking and waiting for the right time to strike," said Dee, her voice quaking with fear and concern.

"Exactly," Ms. Revel confirmed.

"Excuse me," Makenna cut in, coughing slightly. "Would someone like to tell me what's going on?"

Ms. Revel leveled an urgent glare at her, which made Makenna feel uneasy and more than a little afraid.

"Listen carefully, child. We may not have much time. That worm, Fluffy as you call him, was no friend. You were right, he is a double agent, but he is not working for our side. He made you think he was working for us, but in fact was working for the forces of evil."

"Oh no! what have I done?" Makenna exclaimed. Fluffy had seemed so nice. She felt a sense of nausea overtake her. "I'm not helping the twins, I'm making it worse!"

Ms. Revel grabbed Makenna's face in both hands and leaned close, looking directly into her eyes. "Now hush, Virago, and listen. He is known as the Lord of Lies, the King of Deceit. He has been practicing his Dark Arts since the dawn of creation. You child, by comparison, have been the Virago for mere seconds."

"And I might add, have performed extremely well," added Dee Delphine.

Bree chimed in, "Yes, you have! You took on a Hound in your first battle and defeated him. That's very impressive."

Marigold continued, "Makenna, we must deal with things as they come. We will deal with this." To the two hovering fairies, she said, "Bree! Dee! Put out an emergency call to the Fairy Concilium. I want as many sisters and brothers as are available, as well as yourselves, to patrol the area for Alghanii."

"Ma'am...?" Dee asked.

"I know, Dee, they are not going to make themselves easy to spot, but I want to be alerted the minute anyone notices anything out of the ordinary."

"Yes, ma'am," the fairy cousins answered in unison.

Ms. Revel turned back to Makenna. "Now, Makenna, I want you to try to find this... Fluffy. Let's get to the bottom of this, shall we?"

"Yes, ma'am," answered Makenna. She felt very much betrayed by her supposed little friend.

"What are you waiting for, ladies?" Ms. Revel addressed Bree and Dee. "Get to the Concilium now...go!"

Both Bree and Dee realized there was no time for pleasantries. As quickly as they appeared, they were gone.

Less than a minute later, Makenna was in her backyard, calling for her two-faced friend. "Fluffy, Fluffy, where are you?" Now back in her fairy form, Marigold flew outside after her, then hovered just out of sight.

"What's up, kid?" answered the earthworm, popping his head out of the grass. "I'm trying to take a dirt nap here."

"Oh, there you are, Fluffy. Didn't you see it?" she asked. "I kicked one of those Hound's butts."

"I didn't see, it but I heard about it," Fluffy answered. "Nice work." Marigold had heard enough. She was in no mood to be fooled with.

She was Marigold Frith, Fairy Prelate, and she was angry. So angry, in fact, she began to emit a red glow as she swooped down upon the hapless earthworm and plucked him from the soil. "I'll bet you heard about it!" She gestured at a nearby poplar tree. "Give me one reason why I shouldn't drop you in that robin's nest to become a tasty snack for her younglings!"

Fluffy squirmed in her grasp, all pretense falling away. "Please... Please, I had no choice!" he begged.

"Not good enough!" Marigold began to fly the worm closer and closer to the bird's nest. "Those baby birds look quite hungry, worm."

"Wait...wait please! What about due process, a fair trial, Miranda rights, presumption of innocence?" he pleaded.

"What about those hungry birds?" asked Marigold.

In the nest, a trio of hungry birds peeped excitedly, anticipating their next meal.

"Hold on, Marigold," Makenna said, stopping Marigold mid-flight. "Bring him to me."

"Yes, Virago," Marigold flew the terrified worm back down to Makenna and dropped him into Makenna's open palm.

"Hey! Take it easy there! That hurt," Fluffy grunted as he hit Makenna's hand.

"Don't try my patience, worm!" warned the fairy.

Fluffy collected himself and lifted his head up toward Makenna. "You understand, don'tcha kid? The big guy down there put out the word that if we saw anything suspicious anything at all, to let him know. He promised that anyone who gave him a good tip would be taken care of and lead a very pampered life. You don't know what it's like down here in the dirt! It's a worm-eat-worm world. It was just too sweet a deal to pass up. Anyway, I was in the bushes that day when I saw you rescue your Dad at the hospital. At that moment, I knew I hit pay dirt. I knew you were the one. I put the word out that they may want to send a Hound to investigate. I guess they listened. I'm sorry, kid."

"Fluffy, I really thought we were friends," Makenna said, furrowing her brow in disappointment. "You hurt me, and what's worse you could have gotten us all killed. Was it all worth it?"

"Aww...kid, don't start with the guilt-trip, please," Fluffy said. "Give me a break. I think I'd rather end up with the birds."

"That can be arranged," Marigold said with a scowl.

"I even named you after my favorite stuffed animal," Makenna said. "We can't let him go, Virago," Marigold said, firmly. "We need to find out what he said and to whom he said it. We also have to prevent him from talking to anyone else."

"What else did you tell him, Fluffy?" asked Makenna. "Nothing, kid, I swear... I ..."

"We can't trust him, Virago." Marigold cut in. "For all we know, the Alghanii are here already, thanks to that worm." Marigold spit out the word as if it were a curse.

"Alghanii? What are Alghanii?" asked Makenna.

"They make the Hounds look like baby Cocker Spaniels!" exclaimed Fluffy. "They make Darth Vader look like Gandhi... they make..."

"HUSH, creature, before I personally deliver you to a bait shop!" Marigold warned.

"I'm telling you, kid, I only tipped off the Hounds," insisted Fluffy.

Marigold turned her attention to Makenna. "Even if the worm is telling the truth and he really did only alert the Hounds, that may well be enough to give us away. I cast a cloaking spell after the Hound in the park attacked you. If anyone connects the worm's alert to the Hounds with any alarms set off by your battle, even if I cloaked it ...well, the Evil One is no dummy. We cannot underestimate him. We would be foolish to assume anything but that the Alghanii are on their way, or already here! All thanks to your slimy little friend."

"Marigold, what are Alghanii?" asked Makenna again, this time with more persistence.

"They are his minions. Assistants, if you will. The Evil One prefers to have others do his bidding, rather than do his own dirty work. It is too risky for him to come out in the open and expose himself to the light. He sends others."

"And what are these Alghanii like?"

"The worm is correct," Marigold replied. "They are formidable, evil demons. But you have already proven to be quite formidable yourself, Virago."

Makenna remembered her lesson from earlier that day, with Mr. Rose. President Roosevelt's words echoed in her head. "The only thing we have to fear is fear itself." Makenna kept repeating it in her head, hoping the words would sink in deep enough to suppress her fears.

"Uhmm, I don't mean to be rude here, ladies," said Fluffy, sounding uncomfortable, "but do I have to be here for this?"

"You're right, worm, you don't have to be here." Marigold made a move to pick him up again.

"Marigold, wait! One thing at a time," said Makenna. "I have a jar in my room. For now, we'll put Fluffy there, and I'll keep him as a pet. This will stop him from doing any more harm. Let's check back with Bree and Dee and see if they've heard anything on these Alghanii."

"A PET?!" exclaimed Fluffy in protest.

Makenna glared at him. "Either be a pet or bird's breakfast. What will it be?" she snapped.

14

THE ARRIVAL

The limousine pulled off Sunset Boulevard and into the half-circle driveway of the trendy Mondrian Hotel. The limo stopped in front of the double glass-door entranceway.

The valet opened the car door and two exquisite women stepped out. The duo of six-foot-tall women cut an enviable path as they entered the foyer. Both were clad in expensive looking, well-tailored navy suits. They made such an impression that some of the ever-present paparazzi began to snap pictures, figuring that these extraordinary women had to be important. Ms. Creante and Ms. Chevious were seemingly unaffected and unimpressed by the buzz they created as they made their grand entrance. They proceeded to the front desk as all eyes watched them.

The desk clerk greeted them with a smile. "Good morning, ladies. Welcome to the Mondrian Hotel. How may I help you?"

"Good morning," said Ms. Creante. "We have a reservation booked under the name of Seaton."

"Yes, indeed. Sir Seaton has reserved our finest suite for you ladies," answered the clerk. "Everything has been taken care of. The porter will take your bags, and here are your room keys."

Suddenly, the din in the lobby increased tenfold. The atmosphere became electric. Cameras were flashing and snapping, and paparazzi were buzzing around the hotel entrance like a swarm of bees. The women turned their attention in response. The subject of all the chaos could hardly be seen through the horde of photographers that engulfed them.

"What seems to be the trouble?" Ms. Creante asked the clerk, confused by the commotion.

"Oh, no trouble," the clerk answered. "It's just the arrival of Brent Barr and his new wife, Anjennette Jones."

"Who?"

The clerk's eyebrows raised, giving them an 'are you serious' look. "Brent Barr! He's only one of the most famous actors in Hollywood. His recent break up from Jillian Atworthy and marriage to Anjennette Jones has been in literally every tabloid in the world. They just announced that she is pregnant with his baby, although the tabloids have been predicting it for months. They're here for a press conference to discuss the announcement of the pregnancy."

"Oh yes...I think we've heard of them," she said, smiling at Ms. Chevious. "Thank you very much, uhmm ...your name is?"

"Peter," the clerk said, summoning the bellhop to escort the women to their room. "By the way, your bags should already be in your suite, ladies." "Yes, thank you Peter," she answered, handing him two crisp hundred-dollar bills.

Ms. Chevious looked over at her partner, smiled roguishly and winked. "let's have some fun, shall we?"

Ms. Creante returned a knowing smile.

The two women crossed the lobby of the Mondrian, cutting a notice-able path, even over the ruckus caused by the celebrities' arrival. The ladies set a direct course for the Hollywood star and his starlet bride, both of whom stood at the elevator doors, waiting to go up to the pressroom. They were soon joined by the two new hotel guests, on their way to their penthouse suite.

Ms. Chevious looked over at Brent Barr and shot him a quick, fetching smile; a smile that any red-blooded American male would fall prey to. The actor returned the favor, flashing a grin that had obviously been rehearsed in front of a mirror for years. He was a good-looking man, with wavy, collar-length blonde hair, sparkling blue eyes, perfect white teeth, dimpled cheeks, and a cleft in his chin. He wore a tight black t-shirt that outlined a well-cut physique, along with a pair of ripped jeans and Gucci flip-flops.

As perfect a human male specimen as he is, Ms. Chevious thought, *he is still only a mere human.*

The actor's response to Ms. Chevious did not go unnoticed by the surrounding paparazzi and, more particularly, by his wife. The actress squeezed her husband's hand, subtly shooting him a look of disapproval.

The elevator doors opened, and the pregnant Mrs. Barr-Jones began to enter. She felt her husband's arm across her chest, blocking her and effectively preventing her from entering. Mr. Barr smiled at the women, nodding at them to proceed into the elevator first.

As Ms. Chevious entered in deference to the actor's gentlemanly gesture, she whispered to Ms. Creante, "I just love Los Angeles; they spend so much time on their bodies and so little time on their souls."

Ms. Creante chuckled in response.

15

THE NARROWING

The next day, the ladies were in their suite, poring over maps of the greater Los Angeles area, when the phone rang. Ms. Creante answered it. "In Los Angeles only twenty-four hours and already creating havoc?" a voice asked. "I couldn't be any prouder."

"I don't understand, sir," said Ms. Creante. "You obviously haven't seen today's tabloids." "No, sir."

"Let me read you the headline in today's *Inquisitor*," he said,

sounding delighted. "The article was brought to me by one of the staff. To begin with, there's a lovely picture of the two of you entering the elevator at the Mondrian, while some Hollywood actor holds back his very preg- nant wife to allow you entry. The headline reads 'ANJEN-NETTE EXCITED ABOUT ARRIVAL OF NEW BABY, BRENT EXCITED ABOUT ARRIVAL OF NEW FEMALE GUESTS'. The subheading

reads, 'Is the Marriage Already Over?' You must see this woman's face in the picture. She's trying to hide it, but she's furious. Nice work, ladies. This smacks of Ms. Chevious' handiwork."

"Right again, sir," Ms. Creante confirmed. "How goes the mission?"

"The Efflusyum levels are spiking," Ms. Creante replied, "and we are getting some exceptional readings. They show some anomalies, however. Ms. Chevious and I are will be heading out shortly to track down the source."

"Excellent, Ms. Creante," he said, sounding even more delighted. "We'll keep you posted, sir."

"Say hello to Ms. Chevious for me, and commend her on her fine work," he said just before hanging up.

Ms. Creante approached her partner, looking over her shoulder as she sifted through the maps strewn across the bed. "Where to next?"

Ms. Chievous smiled. "Pasadena."

16

THE TRAITOR

Makenna lay in her bed, wide awake. She was painfully aware of the traitor on her nightstand, carefully sealed in a mason jar with several small holes poked in the lid.

She couldn't take it anymore. "Seriously, Fluffy, how could you? I mean, never mind me, what about Emi and Noah? They're innocent babies, for Pete's sake!"

"I'm sorry, kid. I know I screwed up," came Fluffy's voice, muffled through the glass jar.

Makenna sat up in bed, underwhelmed and upset by the worm's response. "Don't just say that, Fluffy. I know what you're trying to do. You're not getting out."

"It's not so bad in here. Trust me, I'm a lot safer here than out there right now. Once the powers that be find out I snitched, I'm dead anyway."

"Oh boo-hoo, like I'm supposed to feel sorry for you. That Hound almost ripped me apart! And while we're on the subject, who or what is this Dark One or whatever his name is? What does he look like? Where does he live?"

"There are rumors, whispers, that kind of stuff. No one in the know is gonna share that kind of information, certainly not with a mud-dweller like me. I'm as low as you can get on the totem pole. I do know this much: he has minions to do his bidding. Doesn't like to get his hands dirty. Besides that, he can change shape or form at any time. It's impossible to tell who or what he really is."

"Spoken like a true traitor." Makenna slammed her body back in her bed and pulled the covers up, frustrated by Fluffy's answer. "Let me guess: you don't know anything about these Alghanii either!"

"Honestly, I heard about 'em, just never seen 'em. All I know is they're very nasty demons."

"Thanks a lot, Fluffy. You've been a huge help. Good night."

17

THE CONTEST

It was a beautiful California day at the Burbank Skateboard Park. The sky was blue, the sun was shining, and the temperature hovered around a comfortable seventy degrees. It was just the kind of day Makenna needed to relax and not dwell on the fact that these Alghanii, whatever they were, could be approaching.

The skate park was awesome, and surprisingly empty for such a perfect day. It featured a large bowl for skaters and a spine leading out to the reservoir section. Along with all the expected standard features, the reservoir was splattered with a pyramid and some alcove transitions.

Surrounding the concrete skater bowls was a breathtaking vista of trees and lush green grass, complete with picnic areas. This provided the opportunity for people to relax and eat while watching some serious and challenging skateboarding action.

Makenna, as usual, was practicing her maneuvers on the Low-rider. Today was a little more special than others, because her new friend Stephen had joined her. Her Dad picked Stephen up from his house so both he and Makenna could enjoy the great California day.

In contrast to Makenna's Low-rider, Stephen opted for roller blades, a hockey stick, and a ball. He was enjoying the course, Canada-style. Both

Makenna and Stephen, were impressed by each other's skills on their chosen modes of transportation. To Makenna's surprise, Stephen really knew how to maneuver on his skates. He shot the ball around, bouncing it off the wall of the bowl and catching the rebounds. He showed Makenna the difference between a slap shot and a wrist shot. Makenna was impressed, as was Stephen when Makenna showed him the finer points of a nose grab.

Stephen talked about his life back in Toronto, and Makenna gave him the inside information on the kids at school, and on life in California. Makenna made certain to warn Stephen about Heather and her gang, but Stephen said he already sensed trouble from the moment he laid eyes on her, which pleased Makenna to no end.

The two friends had no sooner finished their discussion about Heather and her brood when they heard the trademark sneer that could only belong to the notorious Heather Stern.

"Well, look who it is," she called from the upper deck of the stands. "The new school couple. Really, Stephen, you're new here so I guess I can understand. You obviously have a lot to learn about California social skills. You have to be careful who you associate with."

Stephen ignored the comment, continuing to bank shots off the wall as he skated around the bowl.

"Always a pleasure, Heather," answered Makenna.

"I see you're on that ridiculous Low-rider again," Heather jeered. "Seriously Makenna, you'll go to any lengths to prove you're better than me. When will you realize it's just not going to happen? I've won the Los Angeles County skateboard regionals for the last two years. Using that two-wheel contraption isn't going to get you any further. As a matter of fact, you both can watch me practice for next Saturday's regionals. I'll show you how it's really done, Stephen."

"No thanks," Stephen said, sounding genuinely uninterested.

It's time to put Heather in her place, thought Makenna. This time Makenna knew she could win. Makenna was finally going to shut Heather's mouth for good!

"Where can I sign up?" Makenna said defiantly.

"*You?* Compete in the regionals? Oh, this is great!" Heather exclaimed. "Heather Stern gets to beat Makenna Gold yet again! I love it! I just love it!" She stopped crowing for a moment, pointing at the far side of the park. "Sign-up sheets are on a clipboard by the water fountains, over there at the check in. The entry fee is $40.00. And by the way, they've opened the competition to Low-riders, just like yours."

"Don't worry, Heather," Makenna said with feigned politeness. "I'll be there. We'll see who wins this time."

Makenna was excited. It took all her willpower not to say anything about the board being her Armasword. She couldn't wait to show Heather what she could do on it.

18

THE QUICKENING

"Status report, Ms. Creante," Seaton whispered into the phone from his penthouse office high atop the London skyline.

Ms. Creante took a small bite of her chocolate caramel soufflé. She and Ms. Chevious were sitting at a table at a cafe outside the famous Mi Corleone restaurant in Old Town Pasadena. Ms. Creante savored the flavor of the decadent dessert.

"This whole area stinks of good. It's rather repellent," she answered. "Be that as it may, our sensors seem to indicate that the Gift is close."

"Excellent, Ms. Creante," Seaton said. "Slight anomaly, however."

"Proceed," he ordered.

"I'm not sure if it's our sensors, but sometimes it registers as if there is more than one source. Almost as if there is more than one Gift."

"Interesting. What is he up to?" Seaton pondered. Ms. Creante sensed just the slightest hint of nervousness in Seaton's tone. Not that she would ever mention it to him.

Seaton changed the subject. "And how is Ms. Chevious?"

"She's fine, sir. All seems to be proceeding well. We should be able to locate and isolate the Gift in no time."

"No doubt he will have assigned the Gift a protector," Seaton mused.

"Show no mercy. Let's make an example of whatever unlucky soul got the job."

"Done, sir," Ms. Creante answered. Ms. Chevious nodded and smiled back at her as if she had somehow sensed Sir Seaton's mandate.

"I will talk to you soon, ladies," Seaton said, then hung up.

At that moment, a middle-aged, somewhat overweight woman seated at an adjacent table leaned over to Ms. Chievous and politely asked, "How can she eat those desserts and keep that figure?"

Ms. Creante smiled wryly at her partner. "She offsets the sweets by eating extraordinary amounts of protein."

"Whatever do you mean, dear?" the woman asked. "She eats men for lunch."

The woman laughed lightly. "Oh darling, you are very funny."

Ms. Creante looked the woman squarely in the eye and, in a deadly serious tone replied, "No really! She eats men for lunch."

The woman awkwardly turned back to her table. Ms. Creante smirked roguishly at her partner.

19

THE SET-UP

Both Makenna and Stephen were worn out from the morning's activities. They sat in silence, in the back seat of her Dad's car. It was Stephen who broke the silence.

"Heather set you up, you know." Makenna sighed. "I know."

"She knew you would take the bait and sign up for the competition." "I know."

Stephen flashed a smile, complete with dimples. "Don't worry, you're gonna kick her butt!"

"I know," Makenna said again, this time with a smile. It felt nice to hear someone encourage her like that, especially a cute boy she was beginning to like.

After dropping Stephen off at his house, Makenna moved to the front seat next to her father.

"Wow, baby," said Dad, "I'm so excited for next week. I couldn't believe it when you asked to enter that competition. We'll all be there to cheer you on. Me, Mom, Ms. Revel, and the twins. I can't wait to see you on that Low-rider. You're gonna do great."

Makenna's stomach flipped. Noah and Emi out in the open, in public, in a crowd! *Bad idea*, she thought. But she couldn't pull out of the compe- tition now – she'd never be able to face Heather again.

"Dad, maybe it's better if just you come next week," she said. "After all, it's my first competition and... well, with everyone there, I might be too nervous. Plus, the babies could get sick."

"Nonsense!" he answered. "You're great on that thing. Besides, no matter what happens, we're going to be there rooting for you as a family."

As her Dad's car pulled into the driveway, Makenna's stomach flipped again. *Oh no. What's Marigold going to say?*

Makenna didn't have to wait long for the answer. As soon as Ms. Revel was invited to the competition, she quietly pulled Makenna into her room.

"What in the stars were you thinking?" she asked. "Entering a skate-board competition? Drawing attention to yourself? Bringing the twins out into the open! We don't know how close the Alghanii are, and you're making it easy for them, child!"

"I know! I'm sorry! Heather put me on the spot – she challenged me. Before I knew it, I was signed up," Makenna explained. "This whole Virago thing takes a little getting used to."

Ms. Revel's face softened, realizing she might have been overly harsh. "It's all right, Makenna. I will inform the Concilium so we can take the proper precautions." She offered Makenna a hug. "For all this trouble, you'd better win that competition! Oh, and one more thing: no flying! We don't need all of Pasadena and Burbank asking where they can get their own flying Low-rider!"

Makenna laughed. "I promise, no flying. And I promise I'll win!"

The two were interrupted by a knock at the door. "Come in, sir," Ms. Revel called.

"How'd you know it was me?" asked Makenna's father, appearing in the doorway.

"Just instinct sir, you have a very distinctive knock," she answered. "Oh," he said, looking bemused. Makenna just giggled. "Well, I hate to interrupt you ladies," he continued. "Makenna, you know I don't mind if you have pets in the house, but we agreed I have to okay it first."

"What are you talking about, Dad?" Makenna asked.

"That earthworm in your room, young lady," he answered, slightly irritated.

Makenna had forgotten about Fluffy. "Oh right, the earthworm," she answered, her mind racing "Well, he's not really a pet. I just need to observe him for a few days for, um... a science project."

"Oh. I wish I'd known that." He looked at his feet. "Why? What's wrong, Dad?"

"Well... I sort of let him go," he said, his face reddening. "**What**?!" exclaimed Makenna and Ms. Revel simultaneously.

"I'm sorry," he said, sounding embarrassed. "I assumed you had taken in a pet without asking and he looked like he wanted out. I felt bad for him. You should have seen him clinging to the side of the jar. It was like he was begging to be let go, so I set him free. But it shouldn't be that hard to find another worm out there in the garden."

"I know, Dad!" Makenna began to pace back and forth. "But this worm was different."

"I don't understand. Different in what way?"

Ms. Revel chimed in. "It was an honest mistake. Your father is right, Makenna. I'm sure you'll have no trouble finding another earthworm for your project."

"But, Ms. Revel..." Makenna began.

"Pish posh, child," she cut Makenna off. "I'll help you get another one. Now enough talk of this, let's go outside before it gets too dark to find one."

"I'll leave you ladies to your worm-hunting," he said, closing the door behind him.

When her father was gone, Makenna turned to Ms. Revel. "He let Fluffy go. This makes things even worse. What do we do now?"

"This Low-rider competition of yours promises to be very interesting," Ms. Revel said as calmly as she could.

20

THE DAY BEFORE

"Are you ready for tomorrow?" Stephen asked, lunch in hand, as he sat down next to Makenna on the cafeteria bench.

"I guess," Makenna mumbled.

"What's the problem, Makenna? You should be pumped!" Stephen took a bite of his sandwich. "Yer gunna kigger butt," he added, his words garbled by the food in his mouth.

Makenna laughed. "Stephen, it'd probably sound better without a mouthful of sandwich."

"It's just that I'm excited for the competition, why aren't you?" Stephen countered, blushing.

"It's not that. I am excited. But there's so much, I don't know... other stuff."

"What other stuff? We'll all be there to support you. Your entire family is going!"

"Yeah, I know. That's the problem." Makenna said under her breath.

"What? What did you say?"

"Nothing, Stephen. Probably just nerves."

"Seriously?" an infamous voice came from behind them. "You really have time to sit here chatting and eating when the competition is less than twenty-hour hours away? If I were you, Makenna, I'd be out there prac- ticing right now."

"Well you're not me, Heather," Makenna said through gritted teeth.

"Thank God," Heather sneered.

Stephen shot her his meanest scowl. "Makenna's gonna kick your butt."

"As much as I appreciate loyalty in a guy," Heather said, "it's a little misplaced this time."

She walked around behind him, gently running her finger up across his back. It sent chill down his spine, and not the good kind.

"Where are your two tagalongs, Elise and Michelle?" Stephen asked, trying to shake her repulsive touch.

"Yes, where are the bookends?" Makenna teased.

As if on cue, there came a high-pitched squeal from behind them. "Heather! There you are!" Michelle screeched. "Elise and I have been looking all over for you! We never thought we'd find you *here*." She rolled her eyes at Makenna.

"Calm down girls. I was just leaving," Makenna said. "Come on, Stephen, let's go eat our lunch somewhere where the air is clearer."

As they walked away together, Stephen fixed Makenna with an expectant look.

"I'm gonna demolish her in that tournament!" Makenna declared. Stephen smiled.

21

THE ALGHANII

Before Makenna knew it, it was Saturday morning. Makenna's parents and Ms. Revel packed the twins in the minivan, and soon they were on their way to the Southern California Regional Skateboard Competition. Everyone seemed excited except for Ms. Revel who, as much as she tried to hide it, appeared apprehensive. For some reason, in that moment Makenna was able to put all the other concerns behind her: Fluffy's great escape, the Alghanii threat, none of it bothered her now. Ms. Revel marveled at Makenna's ability to dissociate herself from everything. Maybe it was this ability that would help make her a strong and effective Virago.

"Excited, sweetie?" asked her Mom.

"I can't wait, Mom," Makenna replied.

"You're gonna do great. We're all very proud of you." "Thanks."

Minutes later, Makenna found herself in line at the reception desk waiting to check in.

"Hi, Makenna," said a voice from behind her.

"Stephen! Hi!" Makenna said, happily surprised. "Why did you come so early?"

"Are you kidding?" He smiled. "I wouldn't risk missing one minute of you kicking Heather's butt for the world. Besides, after you win this thing, we can hang out. I brought my blades and hockey gear. My parents are over there." He pointed to the bleachers. "They told me that if you wanted to stay after the contest, they'll take you home. That's if your parents can't stay."

"Thanks, Stephen, I'd like that." Makenna was thrilled by all the support. For the moment, she didn't seem to have a care in the world.

The competition consisted of two qualifying rounds and one final round, scored by a five-member panel. Heather, as a former champion, got to skip the qualifying rounds.

Makenna sailed through both qualifying rounds with ease. One judge even noted that she was going to be a very strong contender in her division. Her parents were elated, and even Ms. Revel found herself caught up in the excitement.

Makenna was warming up in the practice area, alongside the other competitors, waiting to be called for the final judging when Heather approached. "I can't believe you actually made it this far," she said as she skated by Makenna. "Your luck won't hold, Makenna. I'm going to win, and you'll still be nothing but a loser."

Makenna ignored the taunts. *It's easy to ignore the teasing when you're riding the most powerful board on earth,* she thought. She smiled and kept riding. She was truly enjoying herself. All thoughts of Alghanii, the Hounds, and double-crossing earthworms, were all but gone. In that moment, she was a normal twelve-year-old again. It felt wonderful.

"Makenna Gold, please check in for the final round," said the voice over the loudspeaker. It was time.

As she left the practice area, she heard Heather's parting shot. "I'll be watching, loser," she said, simultaneously configuring the letter 'L' with her thumb and forefinger over the middle of her forehead.

As Makenna approached the check-in area, she felt a strange but familiar feeling, as if someone had sucked the air right out of the park. Makenna recognized it as the same sensation she had felt just before she spotted the Hound. This thought immediately jolted her back to reality. She was the Virago, and she had responsibilities.

She was overcome by a feeling of nervous nausea. Something was wrong, and she knew it.

Makenna surveyed the park. Everything appeared normal at first glance. Spectators cheering from the bleachers, skateboarders warming up, children playing in the landscaped areas. Nothing seemed amiss.

She looked over at Ms. Revel. When Makenna saw the expression on the Nanny's face, she knew Ms. Revel felt it too. Ms. Revel moved over to the double-stroller in which the twins lay. She stood over it like a mother hen guarding her chicks. She motioned at Makenna to look across the park. Makenna followed the subtle direction, and then she saw them.

Two tall, striking looking women. These women didn't possess a natural beauty like the kind Makenna's mom had. It was a macabre beauty, like the Queen in *Snow White*. They looked completely out of place, standing on the grass in their dark formal suits and heels.

Makenna watched as the women surveyed the park, waving a strange device around. It had a spiral antenna on one end and looked like some kind of bizarre detector.

Again, Makenna heard her name over the loudspeaker, but she ignored it, keeping her eye on the mysterious women. Sensing a confrontation was imminent, Makenna saw the women sweep the contraption in the direction of the babies, then freeze. As Makenna watched, the women smiled, folded up the device and pocketed it. They had obviously found what they were looking for and appeared pleased.

The bizarre duo headed toward the bleachers at a brisk pace, where Ms. Revel was waiting with the babies. Ms. Revel's nervous expression turned to one of visible fear.

Who are these women? Why do they scare Ms. Revel so much?
Makenna wondered.

Makenna quickly cut across the park and intercepted them. She planted herself directly in front of the duo, effectively blocking their access to the babies. "Is there something you need?" she asked, eyebrows raised in suspicion.

"My friend and I are dying to see those cute little babies in the stroller over there," answered Ms. Creante, her tone dripping with contrived sweetness.

"They're my brother and sister. They're sleeping right now, and I don't want anyone to wake them. Maybe some other time," Makenna said firmly.

"We only want to look. I'm certain we won't disturb them." Makenna struck a defiant pose. "I said, stay away from them."

"Twins?" said Ms. Chevious, sounding quite amused. "The Gift is twins? That explains the anomaly in the signal. This makes things even more interesting. Oh, the boss going to love this."

"Makenna Gold, last call for the final round, before you forfeit," came the voice over the PA system.

Makenna caught sight of her parents in the bleachers yelling for her to return to the competition. Ms. Revel was already moving, pushing the stroller away from the bleachers.

Makenna jumped onto her board. "You're not getting to them without going through me."

Both women responded with laughter. "Oh, this is great!" said Ms. Creante. "You? You're the Protector, the Warrior of Warriors, the Defender, the Virago? Wonderful. And I thought that smelly little squire who pulled the sword from the stone was a joke. Does he possibly think some common skater-girl can defeat us?"

Makenna was not amused. She stood her ground. By this time, Ms. Revel had deftly been able to move the twins all the way to the parking lot entrance.

"The Gift!" exclaimed Ms. Chevious, pointing to Ms. Revel across the park. "She's taking it!"

From this point on, everything moved in slow motion.

The women turned from Makenna and raced toward Ms. Revel and the twins. In response, the women ran directly through the skaters' competition area in the bowl, making a beeline for the parking lot, showing no concern for anything but their quest to capture the twins. Makenna followed instinctively as they closed in on the stroller. Makenna picked up her board and gave chase, skating right by the judges' table. As she passed by the judges, Makenna yelled over her shoulder, "Makenna Gold, checking in!" Then she jumped the curb, skated into the bowl, and zoomed out in front of the women, cutting them off.

The perplexed spectators and judges watched the peculiar spectacle unfold.

"Move, Child!" ordered Ms. Creante, "Or you will meet your Creator by day's end!"

Makenna's parents stood staring from the bleachers in disbelief, baffled by what was going on. Stephen was also watching intently, sensing something was terribly wrong.

Makenna stood her ground. "Puh-lease! Whatever!" she said, sounding much more confident than she actually was.

"Time to learn your lesson, child," snapped Ms. Creante. "Meet the Alghanii."

The crowd watched in horror as the women began to morph and grow. As their bodies grew larger, the outer layer of their skin stretched beyond its capacity, like saran wrap been pulled beyond its limits and then ripped apart. The outer epidermis of both women fell to the ground, leaving husks of dead skin discarded on the concrete. At the end of this incredible metamorphosis, two hellish creatures had taken the women's place. They bore no visible relation to anything human. These were demons! They were the Alghanii!

"Ladies and gentlemen," said a voice over the loudspeaker, "this is incredible! This is the most spectacular display we've ever seen in this competition! Makenna Gold is not only skating for us today, she is putting on some kind of show! Let's hear it for those special effects! She's changing the entire nature of the competition! Only in Hollywood, folks. Let's give her a round of applause!"

The crowd applauded with excitement. It seemed they accepted this explanation. Stephen knew better. This was not some elaborately staged production. Makenna was in trouble.

Heather was mortified. She couldn't believe how far Makenna was willing to go to get the judge's approval. "Oh, no way!" she muttered to herself. There was no way she was going to be upstaged by Makenna Gold!

Meanwhile, Makenna stood face to face with the pair of Alghanii. They stood ten feet high and were reptilian in appearance. Their lizard-like hides were an unsightly brownish color. Their arms and legs were pure muscle. Their hands bore only three fingers, with small suction cups at the end of each digit. Their bodies were hunched over, like that of a frog or toad, with large, red, bulbous eyes protruding from their skulls. Alligator-like teeth jutted from their mouths, and a long horn extended from the center of their heads. The Alghanii were a grotesque amalgamation of animals, combining some of their most gruesome features. Literally, beauty had been replaced by beasts.

Makenna continued to stand her ground, although her earlier bravado was giving way to sheer disbelief. She drew herself up in front of the creatures.

"Disgusting!" she muttered.

The Alghanii did not respond verbally. The creatures joined hands, pressing the suction cups of their hands together.

This can't be good, thought Makenna.

As their suction-tipped fingers connected, energy flowed through their reptilian bodies and their hands began to glow with power. Makenna watched, not knowing what to expect, as energy surged from inside the demons. The air around all three of them crackled with static electricity. The Alghanii's clenched hands began to glow brighter and brighter. At that point, Makenna began to suspect what might happen next.

Makenna stomped on the heel of the Low-rider board, sending the board flying up into her hand. She grabbed the board by the central spine, preparing to use it as a makeshift deflector. This time, however, she held the board by the center wheel and spun it. The board rotated rapidly in circles like a propeller at top speed, acting like a spinning shield.

A white bolt of energy exploded from the Alghanii's clasped hands and sliced through the air like a laser beam aimed directly at Makenna.

Makenna held the whirling board up in front of her, kneeling behind it and hoping to deflect the bolt back at the Alghanii as she had done with the Hound. She assumed this tactic would work again. She was wrong.

Instead of deflecting the blast, Makenna was lifted off her feet and flung through the air like a rag doll. The concussive force of the blast was colossal, throwing Makenna back twenty feet. She landed hard against the concrete wall of the skaters' bowl, knocking the breath from her body.

She fell to the ground, panting for air, expecting to feel crushing pain, but there was none. Her indestructible protective gear had absorbed most of the impact, acting like the armor it was meant to be.

Dazed and struggling to recover, she felt like one of Stephen's hockey pucks after one of his slap shots. She fought hard not to pass out.

The crowd gasped in shock as the scene played out in front of them. "My Gosh!" said the announcer over the loudspeaker. "Who put this show together? Stephen Spielberg? Those costumes, that laser blast, that incredible impact that almost looked real! This is stupendous, ladies and gentlemen! Let's give Makenna another hand for putting this production together!"

Makenna focused on the crowds' reaction as she struggled to maintain consciousness.

He parents watched in disbelief as the battle ensued. "Michael, what's going on down there? Did Makenna tell you about this?" her Mom fretted.

"No!" her Dad exclaimed. "I had no idea this was going to happen!" "Something's wrong, Michael! Get down there and help her now!"

Makenna's mother urged. "I'm going to get the babies!" It was at that moment that she noticed that Ms. Revel and the twins were nowhere to be seen.

Not to be overshadowed by Makenna's obvious ploy for attention and over-the-top performance, Heather decided to throw her hat into the ring. She hopped on her skateboard and sailed into the bowl.

"Stop it, creatures," she said, playing along with the drama. "You can't treat my friend like that!"

The Alghanii turned to face the new challenger.

Makenna hadn't fully recovered from the Alghanii blast. Her vision was clouded, her breath coming in shallow pants. All she could muster was a whisper. "Heather, no!"

With all the chaos, there was no way Heather could hear her. Even if she had heard the warning, it was doubtful that she would have listened.

The Alghanii grinned at each other, amused by the child's fool- hardy antics. Heather skated directly toward them. When she was within range of the demonic creatures, one of them reached out a long- suctioned reptilian finger, nonchalantly flicking Heather directly in her face. The force was enough to throw Heather off her skateboard. She hit the concrete floor of the bowl, unconscious before she hit the ground.

The two creatures chortled menacingly.

"Ladies and gentlemen, have you ever seen anything so spectacular in your life?" said the announcer. "Even last year's champion is getting into the act!"

The Alghanii demons crowed in pleasure as they watched the stricken child fall like a sack of potatoes on the concrete. How unfortu- nate that the child was wearing a helmet, which would likely limit her injuries.

At this point, even Makenna was concerned for Heather. She tried to focus her vision, hoping to determine if her rival was still breathing.

It was now Stephen's turn to act. He knew Makenna was in trouble and this was not some elaborate show. Based on what he had just seen the creatures do to both Makenna and Heather, he decided a more indirect approach would be necessary.

He stood at the outer edge of the concrete bowl, placed his puck on the ground, and wound up. He raised his hockey stick high over his head and took aim, preparing to let loose the slap shot of his life. He would have to time his shot perfectly.

Mentally crossing his fingers, Stephen fired off the shot, aiming for the mouth of one of the creatures. The puck moved like a ballistic missile toward its target, zooming into the Alghanii's gaping mouth as the demon cackled.

Stephen smiled in satisfaction as he watched the giant lizard choke and gasp for air, clawing at its own throat. "He shoots, he scores!" he cried, raising his stick over his head in victory.

The second Alghanii looked over at its choking companion, confused. Stephen did not intend to wait around for the creature to figure out what had happened. He ran for cover. Finding a tree close by, Stephen waited behind it for his next opportunity to fire off another shot.

The diversion bought Makenna the time she needed. She needed to take the battle elsewhere. These creatures posed a threat to everyone, and these treacherous demons had no regard for whom they hurt. She was hopeful that Ms. Revel would make sure the twins were out of harm's way. It was time to act.

"Makenna! Makenna!" Her Dad ran toward her, oblivious to the danger he was running headlong into. She had to get the Alghanii out of there, to ensure all the spectators' safety.

She grabbed her board, climbed out of the bowl and climbed on her board. She accelerated toward the parking lot, hoping the Alghanii would follow. She turned her head to see one demon barf up the hockey puck that had lodged in its throat. *Way to go, Stephen!*

The demonic duo collected themselves and spotted Makenna trying to escape. They pursued her, just as she'd hoped. With one leap, their powerful legs carried them out of the bowl and onto the main park path.

Makenna was already halfway to the parking lot. The two Alghanii looked at each other.

One creature said to the other, "You find the Gift, leave the child to me." Then the demons split up.

Makenna had to think fast as the first Alghanii continued its approach. She needed speed and distance, and her Low-rider was her only hope.

At least the odds are better with only one Alghanii on my tail, she thought. One on one seemed more manageable. These things had to have a weakness; after all, Stephen's slap-shot had fazed one of them. Within seconds, she was able to put a hundred feet between her and her Alghanii assailant.

Just then, she thought she heard a familiar voice calling out to her.

Turning her board, she looked around to find the source. Much to her surprise, it was Fluffy, wiggling and moving his head back and forth to try to get her attention, about ten yards away.

"Kid! Kid! Lure that demon over here!" Fluffy cried, poking his head as far over the grass as he could.

Makenna was astonished. She steered her Low-rider down toward the frantic worm.

"Why should I trust you?" she called out.

"I don't have time to explain. Just trust me, please!"

Makenna didn't know why, but something deep within her told her to trust the worm. She decided to go with it.

"Oh, Ms. Alghanii, I'm waiting for you. Come and get me if you can," she called, teasing the beast. The demon, noticeably irritated, took the bait, racing toward Makenna like an enraged bull.

"You better know what you're doing, Fluffy," she whispered.

The Alghanii continued to close the distance between them, but Makenna stood her ground.

"Fluffyyyyyy!" she said anxiously. "Almost, kid, I swear."

When the beast was within ten feet of Makenna, the ground caved in underneath it. The demon sank into the soil as if it had stepped into quicksand. The beast's massive weight and size worked to its disadvantage. The more the creature struggled against the soft mushy soil, the more it became bogged down in the muck and mire.

Fluffy laughed as he watched the beast thrash about. "Kid, me and the rest of the boys down here have been munching through this soil like termites on fresh wood. That thing should be stuck in there for a while. *Now do something!*"

"Thanks, Fluffy," she said, blowing him a kiss.

If a worm could blush, he would have.

Makenna watched as the creature struggled, stuck waist deep in the soil. It was time!

She was the Protector. The Defender of Defenders.

She was the Virago.

Makenna mounted her weapon. She took to the air and skated around to the rear of the beast. She hopped off the board and jumped onto the back of the besieged demon.

The demon swatted at her as if she were a mosquito, but she clung doggedly to its back. Stuck in the soil as it was, the Alghanii's efforts were ineffective.

Makenna acted purely on instinct. She gripped the demon with her legs and held on like a cowboy riding a bucking bronco. As the creature continued to struggle, Makenna noticed a patch of soft tissue just behind its rhino-like horn. She grabbed her board and held it high over her head. The board began to radiate and vibrate with power. Makenna closed her eyes. With all her might, she plunged one end of the board into the soft tissue on the demon's head, piercing its skull.

The Alghanii wailed in agony, a keening cry unlike anything Makenna had ever heard before.

Makenna opened her eyes to see her board embedded six inches deep into the head of the Alghanii demon. The smell was overpowering, making her instantly nauseous. Grayish-green slime bubbled up and oozed from the wound, like lava from a diseased volcano.

With a grunt, Makenna yanked the board out of the demon's gashed head. The creature screamed again. The sound sent chills up and down her spine, and it took a mighty effort to keep from vomiting.

The beast began to sway back and forth.

"Timber, kid!" yelled Fluffy. "That thing's goin' down. Get out of there!"

Makenna jumped off the creature's back. She stepped back a few paces and watched as the beast collapsed. The demon had been defeated, but it didn't feel like much of a win. She was sore, covered in slime, and smelled like she'd been rolling around in cow manure.

Just then, she felt a hand on the back of her shoulder. She spun around, tensing up, ready for another fight.

"Makenna Grace Gold! What in God's name is going on here?" It was her Dad. He looked angry, confused, and most of all, worried.

"Dad!" said Makenna in shock, forgetting that her parents had witnessed everything.

"Yes! Remember me? Watching you fight some ... some... what is that thing?" He pointed to the dead creature buried waist deep in the ground.

As the defeated creature lay in the dirt, it began to smolder, sizzle, and disintegrate before their eyes. Within seconds, all that was left was a black scar on the ground. The rancid smell of burnt meat, ashy residue, and smoke filled the air.

Dumbfounded, her father asked with all the patience he could muster, "Makenna, please tell me what's going here!"

22

THE PURSUIT

"HELP!" The scream came from Makenna's mother. "Somebody stop her! That woman is taking my babies!" In a full-blown panic, Makenna's mother ran toward the parking lot. Even from the distance, Makenna could hear her mother crying through her screams. The chaos continued. The crowd started to make their way toward Misty Gold to see what was wrong.

Makenna turned toward the parking lot. The Alghanii demon had apparently changed back to human form. Ms. Revel was lying motionless on the ground next to a black stretch-limo. Makenna watched as the blonde demon fastened the babies into their car seat, hop into the driver's seat, rev the engine, and peel out of the parking lot. This all happened in a matter of seconds.

"Got to go, Dad!" Makenna jumped on her Low-rider and zoomed toward Ms. Revel.

"Makenna! Where do you think you're... get back here, young lady!

Poor Michael Gold didn't know where to run first.

Makenna ignored her father. It was up to her to rescue Noah and Emi. The explanations would have to wait, and so would the punishment.

She reached Ms. Revel just as the Nanny was picking herself off the ground. "Are you okay?" Makenna asked anxiously.

"I'm fine, dear, but we've got to get those babies. The demon was too much. I couldn't handle her on my own."

Her Dad ran toward them. "Makenna!"

"We don't have much time, Ms. Revel," Makenna said. "What should we do?"

"Bree, Dee... to me, now!" Ms. Revel called out, using Marigold's imperious voice.

The two fairies instantly appeared. "What's happening?" Bree asked.

Ms. Revel held her hands up, calling for silence. "We don't have much time. We've been attacked. Fly over the park immediately, spread an umbrella of memory dust, and then join us back here. Go *now!*"

The fairy cousins obeyed at once.

"Memory dust? What's that?" asked Makenna.

"It will buy us some time," she answered. "It clouds human memories. Everyone who witnessed the last few minutes, including your parents, will suffer a lapse in memory. They will fill in the blanks with their own version of reality. Now enough, we must rescue those babies. We'll need..."

"A car," said Stephen, popping up behind Ms. Revel, car keys in hand.

To Makenna, he was a welcome sight. "My parents drive a Jag. It's right over there. No worries."

"Makenna, we can't bring him! He has no idea of the danger," Marigold insisted.

"I'm already part of this," Stephen said, facing her. "Those things attacked my friend, and now her brother and sister have been kidnapped. We don't have time to argue. Get in the car."

As much as she wanted to deny it, The Fairy Prelate realized the boy was right. They didn't have time to argue. "Let's go," she said.

They were in the car within seconds. Stephen handed the keys to Ms. Revel, who started the car and sat there waiting for something to happen.

"What are you waiting for?" Stephen asked, frustrated and confused. "You do know how to drive don't you, Ms. Revel?" Makenna asked.

"Not to worry, child." Bree and Dee appeared in the car as it idled. Ms. Revel shimmered for a moment, then changed back into Marigold. The three fairies hovered in front of the steering wheel, joined together in a circle, held hands, and began their incantation. "Talutha, Venorum, Mobileum..."

"What the what?" Stephen blurted out, astonished at the sight of the three pixies before him.

Makenna placed a calming hand on his shoulder. "They're Fairies, Stephen. I'll explain as we go."

Struck mute, Stephen could only nod.

The car's transmission shifted into reverse by itself. Marigold looked at Makenna and declared smugly, "It's an animation spell." The blue Jaguar backed out of its spot, shifted into drive, and accelerated out of the parking lot, heading toward the freeway on-ramp.

Stephen was flabbergasted, "Now, I've seen it all! Fairies, self-driving cars, whatever the heck that was back there... What the you-know-what was that?

"Look, Stephen," said Makenna. "It's a lot to take in, and I can't even begin to thank you for all your help back there. I just need to get my sister and brother back."

Makenna faced Marigold. "Where are we going?"

"Realistically, there is only one place the Alghanii would take the twins. And there is only one way to get there. They've got a respectable lead on us, but I think we can catch up to them," said the fairy.

"So, where are we going?" asked a befuddled Stephen.

"There is a little-known entrance ramp right off the 101 Freeway, just west of the 405," answered Marigold. "That entrance ramp merges into another little-known freeway called the Highway to Hell. That's where the Alghanii is taking the twins."

Stephen plunked his body back down into his seat. "What next?"

23

THE CHASE

The Jag expertly weaved in and out of the freeway traffic, as if it were being driven by a NASCAR racer. Darting in and out of lanes, they were averaging 85 mph, but Makenna wished it would go even faster. She wouldn't feel good again until she saw her brother and sister.

Bree noticed the look of concern on Makenna's face. "Don't worry, Virago. We'll save them," she said reassuringly.

Makenna kept her eyes on the road, scanning for the black limo that took her siblings. They had just passed the Coldwater Canyon exit when she saw the limo. It was only a quarter-mile ahead of them. It too, was weaving through traffic like a racecar.

"There it is!" she exclaimed. She was happy, scared, and angry all at the same time. She wanted her brother and sister back, and would not rest until she had them. "Can't this car go any faster?"

"Patience, child," Marigold chided her. "We want to get close enough to get you into range. We don't want to alert the Alghanii of our presence."

Stephen watched and listened quietly, trying to make sense of all that was going on around him. He watched Makenna as she leaned towards the windshield, tracking the limo up ahead. He realized he might be a little out of his league. "Makenna, I know this may not be the best time to ask, but what's going on?"

Makenna looked back at him, momentarily lost for words. "You owe him an explanation child," Marigold suggested.

The Jag swerved sharply to the left, throwing Makenna back into the seat next to him. "Stephen, a lot of this is gonna be very hard for you to believe."

"Makenna, I'm in my parent's car, being driven by fairies and chasing some kind of thing that kidnapped your baby sister and brother. At this point, I think I'd believe anything."

Makenna couldn't really argue with that.

"Quickly Virago." Bree said from the steering wheel. "You won't have time when we catch up to that car."

"Okay, here goes." Makenna let out a deep breath. "Emi and Noah are the hope for this world's future. They are basically here to save humanity. Until they are old enough to do that, I am their protector, along with these fairies."

"And she's very good at it," Dee added.

"I am called the Virago, at least by them," Makenna said, nodding at the fairies in the front seat. "Apparently, the forces of evil have discovered Emi and Noah, and that's why we were fighting them off at the skate park..." She felt herself tearing up.

"Well, why didn't you say so?" Stephen responded with a dimply smile, hoping to coax one out of Makenna. "It's gonna be okay, Makenna. We're gonna get them back and take out that other... whatever that thingy is."

In that moment, Stephen felt a strange determination flow through him. It made him feel confident, brave, strong. He knew, without a doubt, that he and Makenna would be friends forever, and there was nothing he wouldn't do for her.

As the Jag edged closer to the limo, Makenna noticed the license plate. The California plate read EVIL-1. There was no doubt they had the right car. They had just passed the Van Nuys exit and were only minutes away from the freeway overpass.

Suddenly, the limo accelerated, smashing into the cars ahead of it, sending them careening off into the guardrail on the right.

"We've been spotted, kids! Hang on!" Marigold twisted the steering wheel hard to the right.

The limo barreled through the center lane, honking its horn. It surged forward, forcing every car ahead of it out of the way. The Jag followed in hot pursuit, narrowly avoiding the trail of skidding cars left in the limo's wake.

The huge car skidded off to the right-hand lane as if to exit the freeway, but no exit ramp existed. It seemed to be heading straight for the guardrail.

Makenna gasped, fearing for the lives of her siblings. As the limo hit the guardrail, it vanished, leaving only a ripple in the air.

"They made it!" said Marigold, smacking the steering wheel.

"Where did they go! What do we do?" asked Makenna, on the verge of panic.

"We have to follow them."

"Follow what? That car just disappeared into thin air!" Stephen cried. "Hush, boy! Cover your eyes, we're going in!"

"Going in *where*?!" Stephen shouted.

24

THE HIGHWAY TO HELL

"You have *got* to be kidding!" said Stephen. "Just because they were somehow able to –LOOK OUT!!!" Stephen instinctively flinched and threw his hands up over his face.

For a split-second, as the Jag hit the guardrail, the world went pitch-black. It was as if they were driving through sticky tar. Everything seemed to move in slow-motion. Time and space lost all meaning. The entire car, along with its occupants, was covered in a thick layer of darkness. It seemed as if they were engulfed in pure black for what seemed like an eternity.

Suddenly, the car filled with light. They had survived the collision. "Oh, my God!" Stephen gasped, taking a quick inventory of his body
to make sure he was still intact. "What was that?"

Makenna saw the look of terror on her friend's face, feeling bad for dragging him into this chaos. Though she was inexperienced, she'd at least had a short time to adapt to her new role as Virago. Stephen only had minutes. She knew exactly how he felt.

She looked at him again. Even panicked, she couldn't help but notice his pleasant face, smooth skin, rosy cheeks, and bright blue eyes.

"I'm sorry, Stephen," she said.

"It's not your fault, Makenna, I asked to be here," Stephen said, giving her a wobbly smile. "Don't worry, I'm okay. Really."

Makenna smiled back at him. Having Stephen there made her feel better.

Now calmer, Makenna and Stephen both took the opportunity to look out the window.

The scene that met their eyes was nothing short of surreal.

This could be none other than the famous Highway to Hell. It was a broad, four-lane highway, which seemed to descend downwards in a slow, steady decline. There seemed to be only one lane heading in the opposite direction.

The pavement itself consisted of a dull red asphalt. The sky was filled with black and gray clouds against a fiery red-orange backdrop. The air smelled of sulfur, which infiltrated the car through the Jag's air-vents.

"I have a feeling we're not in Kansas anymore," said Stephen. "Maybe if we turn on the radio, it will make us feel better."

Stephen leaned through the gap between the seats and switched on the radio. The song playing was AC/DC's famous hit, "Highway to Hell".

"Oh my God, Seriously?" Stephen muttered. He leaned forward again to change the station but got the same song. In fact, it seemed to be playing on every station. Finally, he gave up and clicked the radio off. "Sorry," he said, sounding disenchanted.

Silence reigned inside the Jag as its occupants peered out through the windows of the car with expressions of shock, disgust, and fear.

Bree shivered. "This is no place for a fairy." "Aye!" agreed Dee.

"Make no mistake, ladies," warned Marigold, "our powers are very limited here."

All the other cars on the road were black, which made their blue Jag stick out like a sore thumb. Additionally, the cars had all tinted windows, making it virtually impossible to see through them.

As Makenna continued to search for the limo, she saw a pack of Harley-Davidson motorcycles just to the right of their car. Riding each one was a skeleton clad in leather and denim. As she gaped, one of the skeleton bikers gave her a toothy smile and a thumbs up.

Makenna, startled, jumped back into her seat and faced away from the window.

"Why do they need helmets?" Stephen asked. "Aren't they already dead?"

"I don't know. Doesn't make sense to me either. Nothing in this place does."

"They are known as Death Riders," Dee explained as if she were a tour guide leading them through Disneyland gone wrong. "They assist the Grim Reaper in his work. Lovely bunch they are."

"There's the limo!" exclaimed Marigold. "Just up ahead."

There it was, up ahead, a limo with the telltale license plate, EVIL-1. "Marigold can we speed up? It feels like the car is driving through sludge."

"Essentially, it is, child. It's the atmosphere down here. We're probably moving as fast as we can, under the circumstances. The rest is up to you, Virago."

"What do you mean?" Makenna asked. She didn't like the sound of this.

"I mean, we can get you close to the car but ultimately it's going to be up to you to get the twins back."

"How am I supposed to... I mean..."

"Trust your instincts, Makenna. I do. I think it was Henry Ford who said, 'whether you think you can or you think you can't, you're probably right'. I trust you Virago, and I know Emi and Noah do as well."

"I trust you too, Makenna," Stephen added.

Makenna knew what she had to do. "Marigold, Bree, Dee, get me as close to that car as you can."

The Jag accelerated, trying to match speed with the limo. When their car was within a few hundred feet of the limo, Makenna opened the car door of the Jag, reeling from the heat that slammed her in the face. It felt like she'd just opened the door to a blazing hot oven. She immediately broke into a sweat, but she had to ignore it. She had no choice.

Makenna grabbed her board, placed it beneath her feet, stood up and pushed off from the moving vehicle.

She took to the air on her Low-rider, feeling like she was flying through a pressure cooker. The air was hot, thick, and stale. The rancid smell of burnt sulfur stung her nostrils. But she would not be deterred.

She willed the board to move faster through the thick, and it responded, accelerating toward the limo.

As she neared the vehicle, she could make out the outline of the infant carrier seats through the rear window.

She had a plan. It was crazy, reckless even, but it was her only shot. Makenna was starting to realize that improvisation was going to be fundamental to her continued existence. She closed in as the limo maintained the same speed, indicating that the Alghanii demon was unaware of Makenna's presence.

She smiled despite the choking heat. The demon probably assumed Makenna lacked the courage to follow it through the Gates of Hell. The demon was wrong!

Makenna began her attack. She jumped off the board and landed on the roof of the moving limo, clinging to it and forcing herself not to cry out. She lay on her stomach, her head just inches from the rear window.

With a deep inhale, Makenna lifted both her hands over her head and smashed her indestructible board into the rear window, causing it to shatter.

Makenna threw the Low-rider into the backseat of the vehicle, knowing she would soon be joining it. She prayed none of the flying glass touched the twins, hoping their car seats had protected them.

The Alghanii hissed, its bulbous eyes were wide with shock. The demon driver looked back as Makenna wriggled head-first through the broken window. With a snarl, the demon wrenched the steering wheel, causing the limo to swerve. Makenna felt her long, thin legs slam into the window frame as the car veered left and then right.

I must get the twins out of here! she thought.

She was so focused on the task at hand, she barely noticed the shards of broken glass cutting through her jeans.

Makenna struggled to keep her balance as the fishtailing car continued to fling her legs against the broken glass of the shattered window. She felt like a pinball in an arcade game, bouncing back and forth.

As Makenna reached down to unbuckle the two car seats, the Alghanii returned to its grotesque demon form. It reached a long muscular arm back, grabbing at her. Makenna held her board up with her left hand, using it as a shield while she continued to unclasp the infant's car seats with her right hand.

The demon struggled to maintain control of the limo, sending it skidding across the red asphalt highway. "Leave the Gift, Virago, they're ours now!" it said. If fire itself had a voice, it would sound like this. "If you give up now, I will let you live."

Makenna ignored the creature. She unclasped one car seat and felt a rush of adrenaline. A few more seconds, and she'd have the other one undone.

"I destroyed one of you already!" she screamed with a firmness she never knew she possessed. "Give me back my brother and sister or be prepared to join your partner!"

She snapped the second clasp open.

Success!

She grabbed both seats by their handles, casting a glance at her siblings to make sure they were both unharmed. Despite the circumstances, it seemed they were both sleeping. *I'm glad they can relax,* she thought to herself. *How ironic.*

Makenna breathed a sigh of relief. She maneuvered her Low-rider under her feet and backed out of the vehicle through the shattered window. Both baby seats in hand, she staved off the flailing fist of the demon as it attempted to thwart her escape.

With one seat under each arm, she veered the board away from the limo, right toward the Jag which continued to keep pace behind them.

Bree and Dee flew out to meet her, flanking her protectively.

"Hand us the twins, Virago! We will get them to safety!" Bree shouted. "You have other things to contend with."

Makenna handed the car seats, with their precious burdens, to the fairies. She watched them fly toward the Jag, swallowing in relief as they handed the carriers to a waiting Stephen. One at a time, he took them and strapped them in.

It wasn't over, but Noah and Emi were safe.

Stephen smiled at Makenna and waved. The Jag then pulled a quick U-turn and jumped the lanes into the single return lane that would lead them out of Hell and back to the physical world.

Makenna's relief was short-lived. The Alghanii was not going to give up that easily, and this time Makenna didn't have Fluffy and his gang of earth-eaters to assist her. From behind, Makenna heard the high- pitched screech of tires from the limousine. Makenna turned in mid-air to meet her adversary.

The limousine skidded around in a U-turn. The Alghanii behind the wheel gunned the engine and jumped the lanes in pursuit of the fleeing Jaguar. The demon had no interest in the Virago. This was about the babies.

The limo accelerated toward the run-away Jaguar. The Jag was moving at a decent rate of speed, but the limousine was gaining. Makenna had to do something to slow the demon's car down.

The limo and the Jag were the only two cars in the Return-to-Reality-Lane. Makenna had to think fast. She knew that even with her Low-rider, she would be no match for an oncoming limousine traveling at breakneck speed. As she hovered over the freeway, watching the limo chase the Jag, she noticed another pack of bikers heading toward them, on their descent to Hell.

Again, improvisation would be what the doctor ordered.

Makenna steered the board in the direction of the bikers. She lifted into the air in a high, graceful arc, yanking the helmet off one of the skeleton Death riders. Unfortunately, she took the biker's head as well. The bike collapsed on its side and skidded along the red asphalt, leaving a six-foot trail of sparks behind it.

"Sorry!" Makenna yelled, regretting the accident she had just caused.

Unfortunately, there wasn't much she could do at this point.

She redirected her attention to the limousine still in pursuit of her brother and sister. Makenna willed the board to move even faster, pushing it harder than she ever had before.

By the time she was close enough to read the EVIL-1 license plate, it was only a few yards from the rear of the Jag. There was no question that if the Alghanii couldn't have the babies, it would destroy them.

Makenna pulled her board alongside the limo on the driver's side, the helmeted skull in her hand.

She glided up the length of the limousine. When she pulled past the front door she pivoted and, with all her strength, flung the helmet into the windshield. The windshield cracked, lines forming in a spider-web pattern from the spot of impact. Makenna prayed this would impair the Alghanii's vision and pursuit.

Makenna's improvised assault forced the limo to slow down. In response, the Alghanii punched its scaly fist through the windshield, disintegrating it. Shards flew out from the vehicle in all directions, including a few that sliced threw the skin on Makenna's right arm like a hot knife through butter. She cried out in pain.

Warm blood ran down her arm, mixing with the salty sweat on her skin. The salt made her injuries burn that much more. It was excruciating, but there was no time to dwell on it. Adrenaline was doing its job and she pushed on.

A half-mile ahead of the Jaguar lay what looked to be a portal or gate- way. Makenna figured this was the door from this realm to the real world. It glowed white, but was too bright to see beyond the entrance.

If they could just make it back to the real world. Makenna felt she might have a better shot at defeating the Alghanii, especially since she already found their Achilles heel: the soft spot at the base of their horn.

BOOM!

The limo rammed the rear bumper of the Jag, trying to force it off the road. Makenna could see Stephen and the fairies tumbling around the vehicle after the impact. The portal was only about a few hundred yards ahead.

Come on! she thought, trying to urge the Jag faster and farther by sheer force of willpower alone.

BOOM!

Again, the limo rammed the Jag's rear bumper. The Jag skidded again, fighting to maintain control.

In the car, Stephen racked his brains, trying to think of anything he could do to help Makenna, while simultaneously trying to shield the twins from any further impact. The twins, surprisingly, gurgled and giggled every time the car took another hit.

BOOM! The car was hit a third time.

"Any suggestions, fairies? We're in trouble!" Stephen asked. "Nothing gets by this boy does it?" said a stressed-out Dee.

Stephen looked out the rear window. Makenna was pulling up alongside them. She gestured up ahead; they were only seconds away from the exit portal. He smiled, relieved that they would soon be out of there. The chase wouldn't end there, but anything was better than Hell.

Makenna grabbed hold of one of the Jag's car door handles, as if she was hitching a ride. The two friends smiled at each other, silently communicating their joint relief. Only a few more seconds, and they would be back in their world.

Stephen looked down at the twins, and his eyes widened. The infants, oddly had reached out their tiny arms and were holding hands. Both were smiling, as if they knew they were going to be all right. For no logical reason, Stephen breathed a sigh of relief. If these babies were as special as Makenna said, then he would trust their instincts. They *were* going to be okay.

Instantly, the world went white. It was as if someone had switched on a thousand-watt bulb inside the car. They had reached the portal.

And just like that, they were back driving northbound on the 101 freeway, as if they had never left. Stephen cast a frantic look out the rear window, anticipating the black limousine would be in hot pursuit.

He waved to Makenna, still grasping the door handle, and motioned behind them.

As they both watched, the guardrail that marked the entrance began to stretch and distort like a rubber band, like something on the other side was pushing unsuccessfully to get through. Stretched to capacity, the guardrail bulged and then snapped back, and the portal contracted back to its original shape. This was followed by was a huge explosion, which seemed to emanate from the portal's center. As the shockwaves from the explosion faded, the portal snapped shut like the iris of a camera. The Alghanii's limo, caught in the vortex of the closing portal, had never made it through.

They were safe!

The car insulated Stephen, the fairies and the babies from the concussive force of the explosion. Makenna was not so fortunate. The force of the blow threw her off her board and sent her flying headlong on to pavement like a twig in a tornado. She hit the pavement hard, bouncing off the concrete several times before finally coming to rest on the 405.

Marigold slammed on the Jag's brakes, pulling onto the freeway's shoulder. Moments later, the fairies flew out of the open windows, speeding toward the unconscious Virago. Cars skidded to avoid her unmoving body.

With forced breaths, Marigold quickly mustered a protective shield around Makenna. Using their considerable fairy strength, the trio scooped her up as gently as they could and flew her back to the waiting automobile. They laid her gently in the back seat of the car, next to Emi and Noah. Her body was a mass of cuts and scrapes. Tears filled the fairies' eyes. Stephen began to tear up as well.

"You have fought well, young Virago," said Marigold.

"She's going to be okay, right?" asked Stephen, tucking a strand of hair behind Makenna's ear.

"Please, oh Great One, make her be okay. She is so special," said Bree. The three fairies flew over Makenna's body, sprinkling their fairy dust, hoping to ensure good dreams and aid in the healing.

The Jag pulled off the freeway. Marigold ordered the car to direct itself to the closest hospital.

25

THE VIRAGO

Makenna lay in her bed, watching television and enjoying a well-deserved rest. It had been five days since the incident, and she had slept for almost three of them. She was still quite sore, but her cuts and bruises were healing. *It wasn't so bad being home for a few days,* she thought. *No Heather to contend with.*

There was a soft knock at the door. "Come in," Makenna said.

"It's me, dearie." Ms. Revel entered Makenna's room with a tray of hot tea and toast. "We must keep up our strength."

"Hello, Ms. Revel," said Makenna, sitting up.

Ms. Revel smiled. "Well, you're looking much better today, Ms. Makenna. You gave us quite a scare, you did."

"I am feeling much better," Makenna responded, then lowered her voice. "But I have a question. I'm worried that... you know, the Evil One, knows where we are now."

"Not to worry, it has already been taken care of. I contacted the Concilium and told them everything. They have already placed small packets of Efflusyum in locations all over the world. That should throw the Hounds off for a while."

Fluffy poked his pink head up through the soil of his new terrarium. "And I have already spread the word underground that you guys have taken off for parts unknown. All indications are that they think you guys are long gone. By the way, kid, thanks for the new crib. Once the man downstairs finds out I helped you out, my life won't be worth the dirt I eat."

"Well I'm glad my Mom and Dad said I could keep you as a pet, Fluffy," Makenna said. "Don't worry, I'll take good care of you."

"I have no doubt."

Ms. Revel placed the tray of food in front of Makenna. "Now that you seem to be more alert, I must caution you: everybody thinks, thanks to some memory dust, that you took a nasty spill at the skateboard competition, caused by a head-on collision between you and Heather. Nobody will have any memory of your battle with the Alghanii which, by the way, is already Legend among the fairies."

"How is Heather?" Makenna asked, marginally concerned. "She's fine. She's no longer the regional champ, but she's fine." "And what about Stephen? Did you erase his memory too?"

"No, child. We thought we'd leave that up to you. We figured he deserved that much. If you want us to erase his memory, we will."

"I guess I'll have to think about that one," Makenna said with a smile. "Oh! I almost forgot to tell you. I named my weapon."

"You have?" asked Ms. Revel, leaning forward in anticipation. "Please, child, don't keep me waiting! What is it?"

"I will call the board... Redeemer," she answered.

"Great name!" Marigold said. "How did you come up with it?"

"Well, it combines in some way, the names of you, Bree and Dee. Think about it: Bree, Dee and Marigold. I take the Ree from Bree, the Dee from Dee and the Mar from Marigold. Switch around a few things and I get, Ree-Dee-Mar, or Redeemer."

"Hey kid, that's pretty good," said Fluffy. "I'm impressed."

"As am I, Virago," said Ms. Revel, blushing slightly. "Thank you, young one. I am honored. I'm certain, when Bree and Dee hear about it, they will be equally grateful."

"Knock, knock! How are you feeling, daredevil?" said Makenna's mom, entering the room.

"Hi, Mom! I'm fine," Makenna said with a smile.

"I'm glad. You know, Makenna, you gave us quite a scare. I don't know if I'll ever want to see you on that thing again."

"Oh Mom, it was just an accident," Makenna answered, looking over at Ms. Revel and winking.

"I just came in to tell you that I have a special visitor here, who wanted to check in on you and see how you were doing."

"Hello, Makenna," said a familiar voice, coming out of a very familiar face that poked through her bedroom doorway.

"Mr. Rose!" Makenna exclaimed. She was very excited to see him. "What are you doing here?"

"I was in the neighborhood, thought I'd check in on my star pupil." He beamed down at her. "So when is my best student coming back to school?

"I think I should be back by..." Makenna looked at her mother and raised her eyebrows hopefully. Her Mom mouthed a silent word that Makenna understood. "Monday." she finished.

"Wonderful," Mr. Rose said. "I look forward to seeing you there."

Makenna's Dad entered the room, a baby in each arm. "I have two babies here who wanted to make sure that their big sissy was okay."

He laid the babies down on Makenna's chest, Noah on her left and Emi on her right. They were as adorable as ever. Makenna looked down at her brother and sister and smiled. They smiled right back. Tears welled up in Makenna's eyes.

"What's wrong baby?" her Mom asked. "Are you all right?" "Happy tears, Mom. Happy tears."

EPILOGUE

"Sir?" said Mr. Xshun over the intercom. "We have confirmed that the Gift is in fact twins, and the Virago is a young girl."

"Excellent, Mr. Xshun," Sir Seaton said, wringing his hands in glee. "When can I expect the arrival of the Gift?"

"Um...sir?" Mr. Xshun asked timidly. "Yes?"

"The Virago destroyed one of the Alghanii, and the other one..." "What?" Sir Seaton thundered, his blood boiling in his veins. "Who destroyed an Alghanii? The child? The girl?" "Yes, sir."

"Do we know where they are?"

"We've lost them sir; the Hounds are still searching. Rumor has it, they have left the area."

Seaton looked down at the chess pawn in his hand. Again, he had accidentally melted the platinum piece into molten slag. "Mr. Xshun, order me another pawn."

The corporate headquarters of Natasi Industries, at Number 66, 6th Street in London, trembled.

UP NEXT!

**Makenna will be Back in The Chronicles of the Virago The Apprentus
Book II**

ACKNOWLEDGMENTS

Special Thanks: Again to my wife, Misty, for her writing input, editing, patience an unyielding belief.

To my parents Esther and Eugene Bialys, for always supporting my creativity. To my other parents, Gregory and Sharon McFern, for trusting me with their most prized possession and always believing in me. To all who in some way helped to inspire me, thank you.

To my Makenna, Emilyne and Noah, my Blessings and My Gift!